W9-CHI-335

STONE ARCH BOOKS
a capstone imprint

STONE ARCH BOOKS™
Published in 2012
A Capstone Imprint
1710 Roe Crest Drive
North Mankato, MN 56003
www.capstonepub.com

Originally published by DC Comics in the U.S. in single magazine form as Tiny Titans #3.

DC Comics
1700 Broadway, New York, NY 10019
A Warner Bros. Entertainment Company

Cataloging-in-Publication Data is available at the Library of Congress website:
ISBN: 978-1-4342-4539-7 (library binding)

Summary: Robin and the boys spend an afternoon in the Batcave! Plus, More Tiny Titans adventures!

STONE ARCH BOOKS
Ashley C. Andersen Zantop *Publisher*
Michael Dahl *Editorial Director*
Donald Lemke & Alison Deering *Editors*
Heather Kindseth *Creative Director*
Hilary Wacholz *Designer*
Kathy McColley *Production Specialist*

DC COMICS
Jann Jones *Original U.S. Editor*
Stephanie Buscema *U.S. Assistant Editor*
Nick J. Napolitano *Letterer*

Printed in the United States of America in Brainerd, Minnesota.
122012 007078R

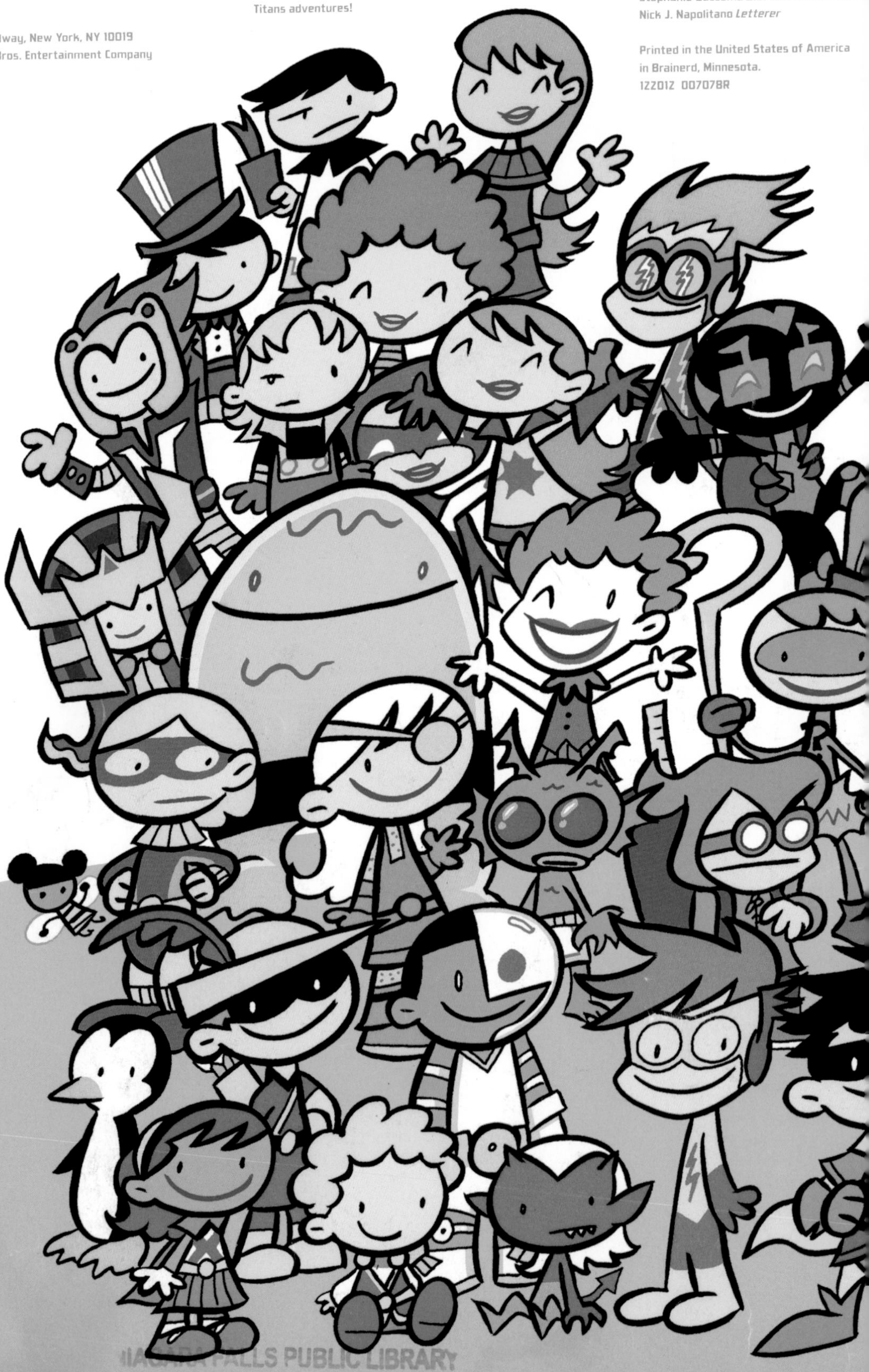

tiny titans

Penguins in the Batcave!

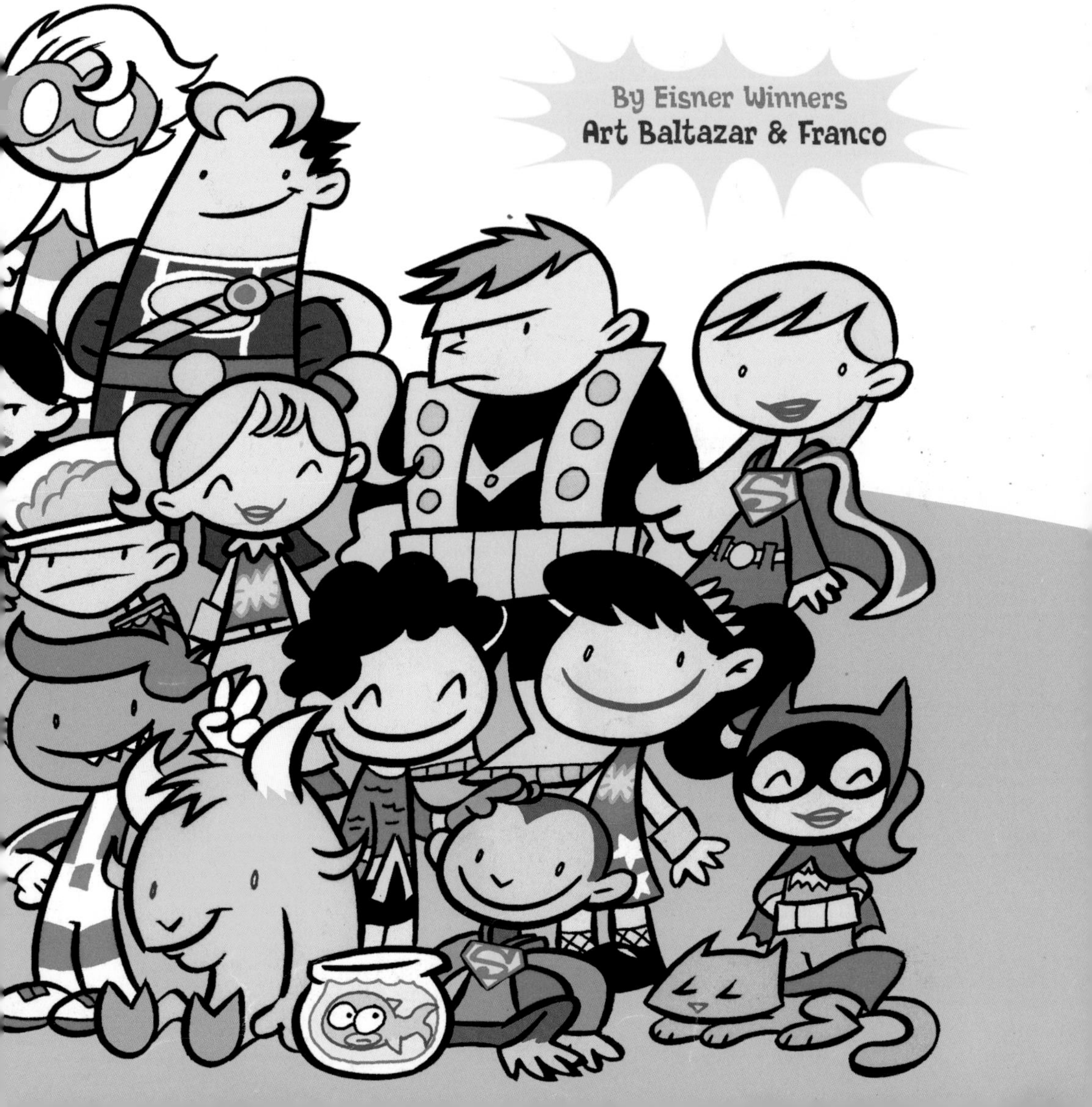
By Eisner Winners
Art Baltazar & Franco

tiny titans

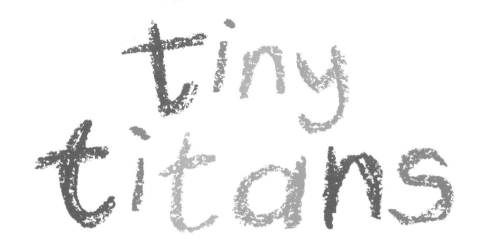

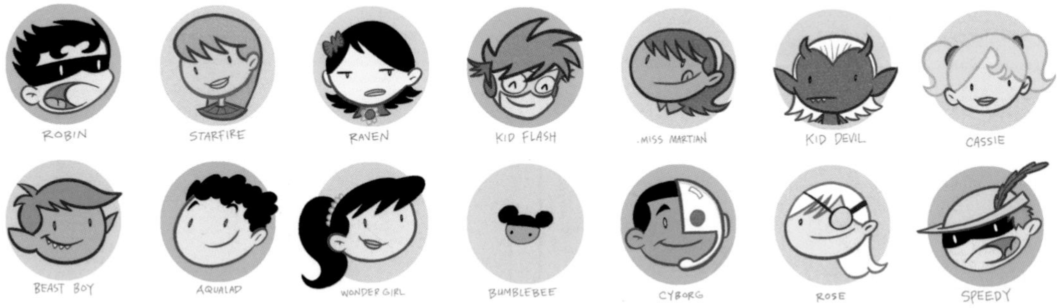
ROBIN
STARFIRE
RAVEN
KID FLASH
MISS MARTIAN
KID DEVIL
CASSIE
BEAST BOY
AQUALAD
WONDER GIRL
BUMBLEBEE
CYBORG
ROSE
SPEEDY

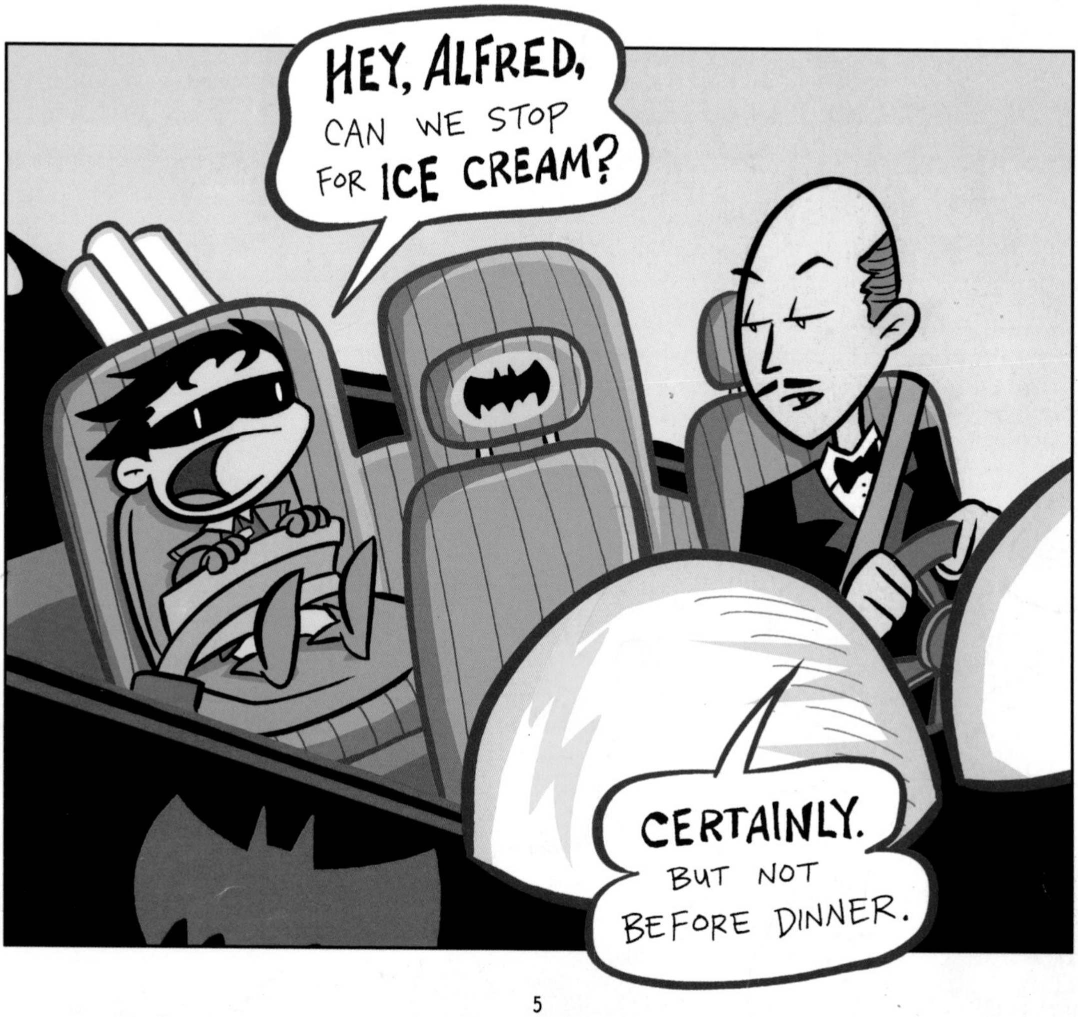
HEY, ALFRED, CAN WE STOP FOR ICE CREAM?
CERTAINLY. BUT NOT BEFORE DINNER.

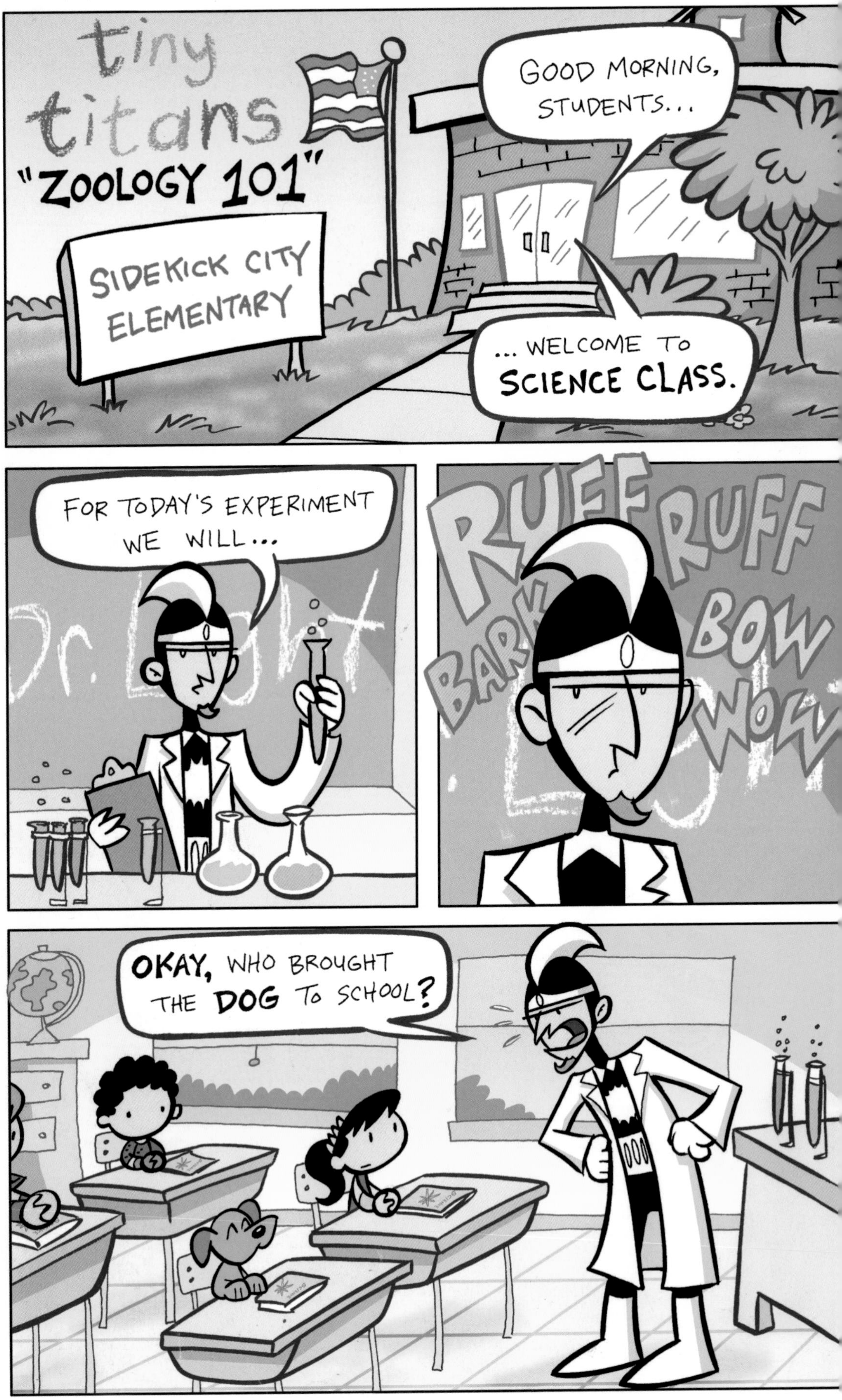
tiny titans
"ZOOLOGY 101"
SIDEKICK CITY ELEMENTARY
GOOD MORNING, STUDENTS...
... WELCOME TO SCIENCE CLASS.
FOR TODAY'S EXPERIMENT WE WILL...
Dr. Light
RUFF RUFF BARK BOW WOW
OKAY, WHO BROUGHT THE DOG TO SCHOOL?

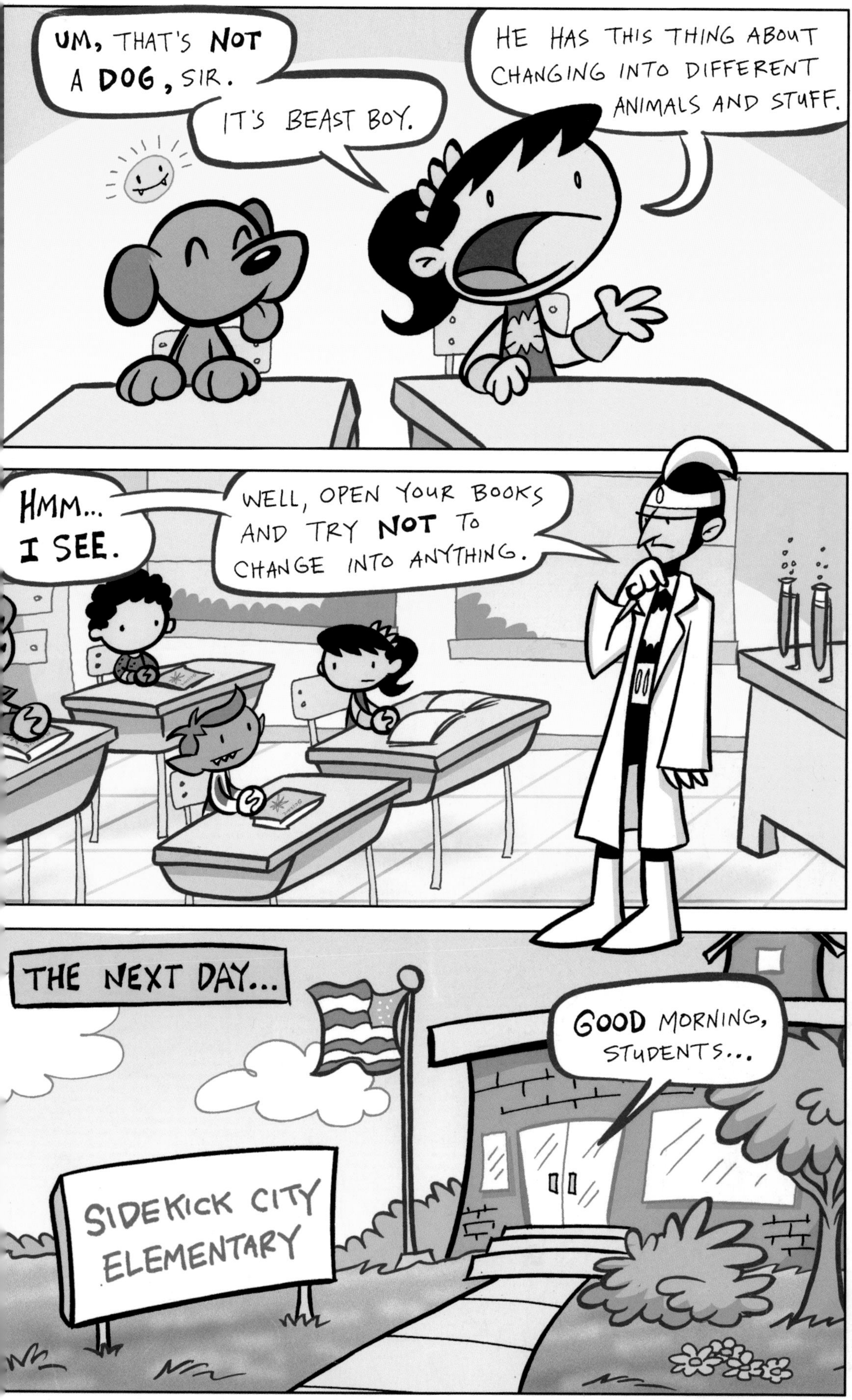
UM, THAT'S NOT A DOG, SIR.
IT'S BEAST BOY.
HE HAS THIS THING ABOUT CHANGING INTO DIFFERENT ANIMALS AND STUFF.
HMM... I SEE.
WELL, OPEN YOUR BOOKS AND TRY NOT TO CHANGE INTO ANYTHING.
THE NEXT DAY...
GOOD MORNING, STUDENTS...
SIDEKICK CITY ELEMENTARY

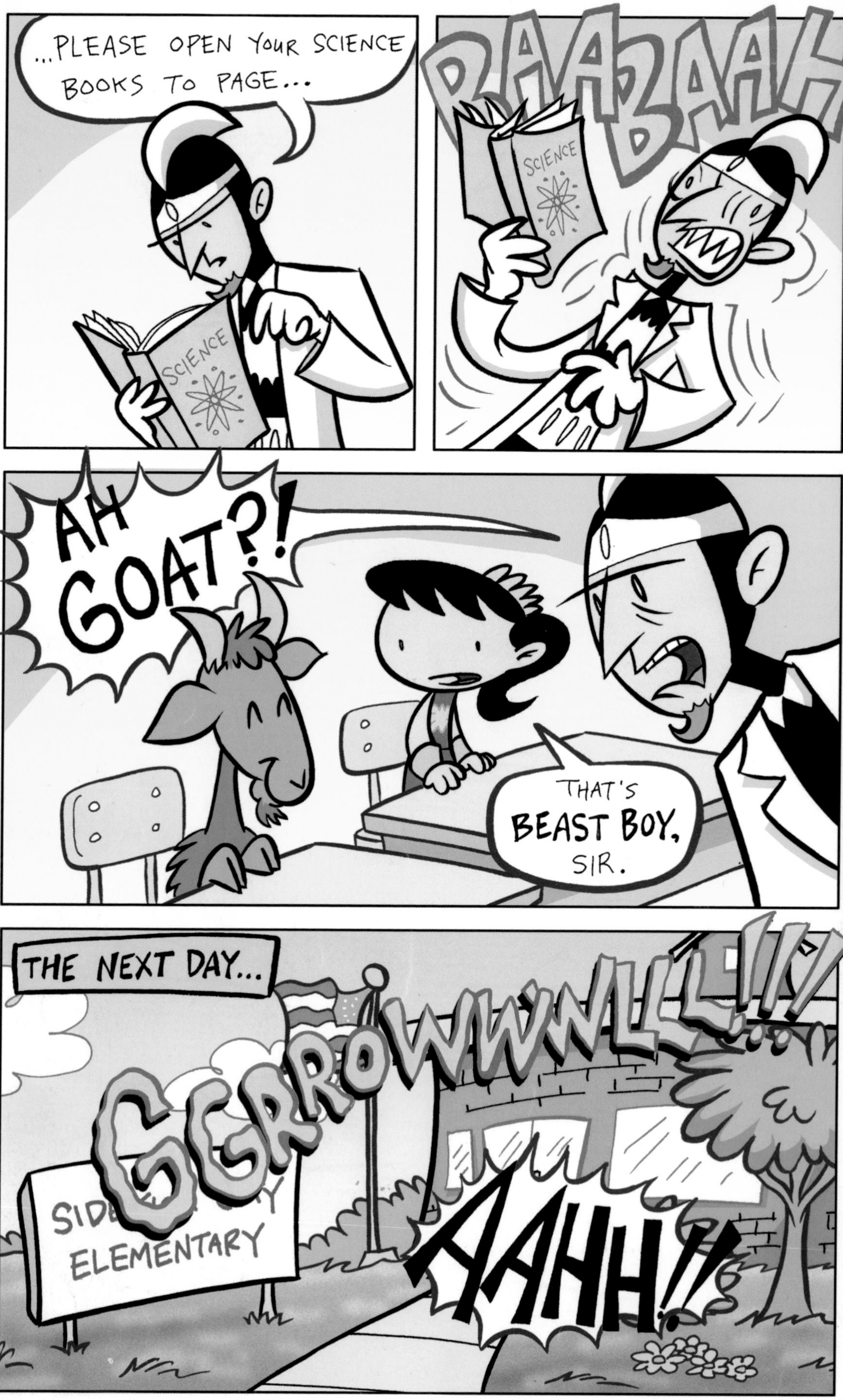
...PLEASE OPEN YOUR SCIENCE BOOKS TO PAGE...
SCIENCE
BAABAAH
SCIENCE
AH GOAT?!
THAT'S BEAST BOY, SIR.
THE NEXT DAY...
GGRROWWWLLL!!!
ELEMENTARY
AAHH!!

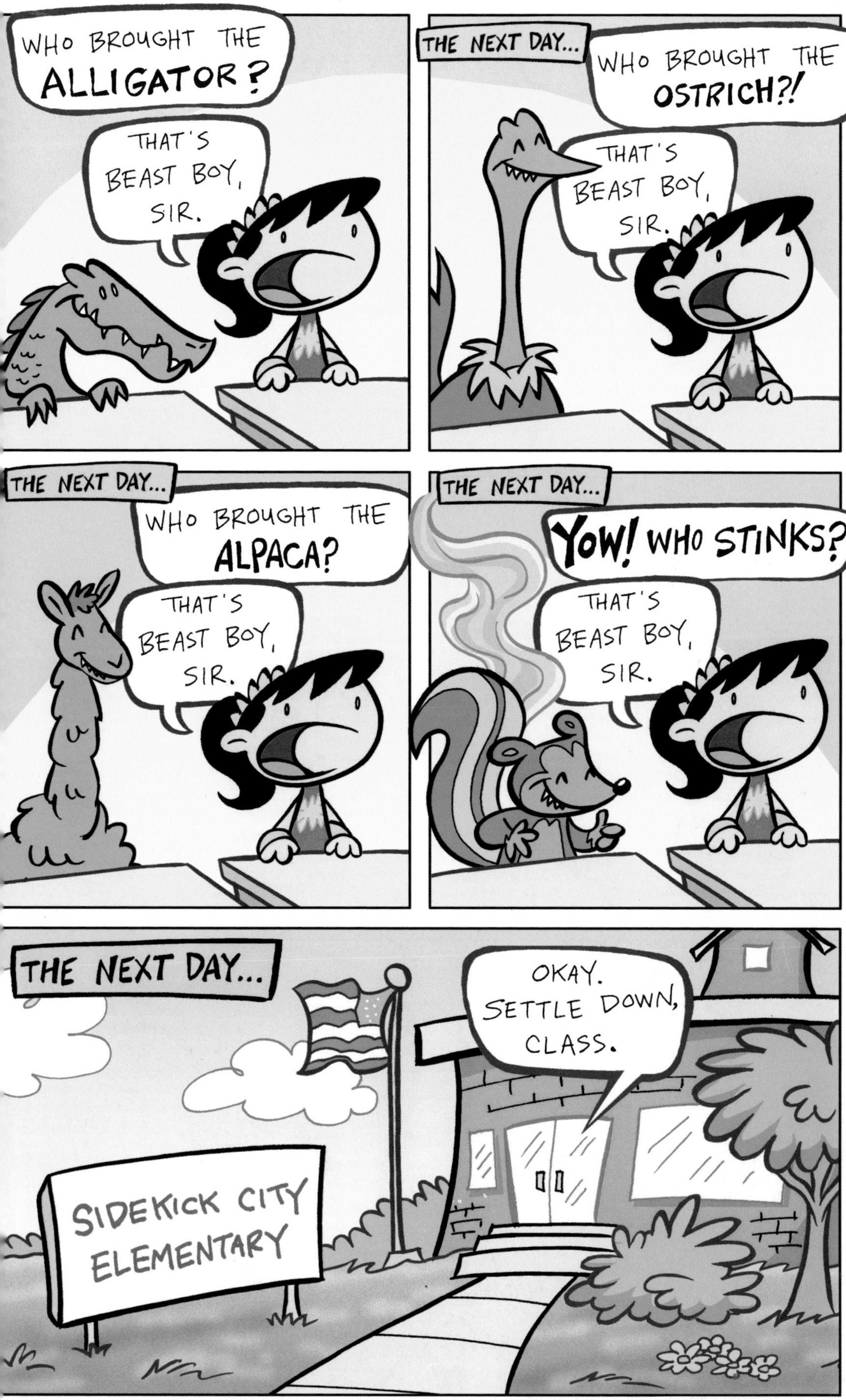
WHO BROUGHT THE ALLIGATOR?
THAT'S BEAST BOY, SIR.
THE NEXT DAY...
WHO BROUGHT THE OSTRICH?!
THAT'S BEAST BOY, SIR.
THE NEXT DAY...
WHO BROUGHT THE ALPACA?
THAT'S BEAST BOY, SIR.
THE NEXT DAY...
YOW! WHO STINKS?
THAT'S BEAST BOY, SIR.
THE NEXT DAY...
SIDEKICK CITY ELEMENTARY
OKAY. SETTLE DOWN, CLASS.

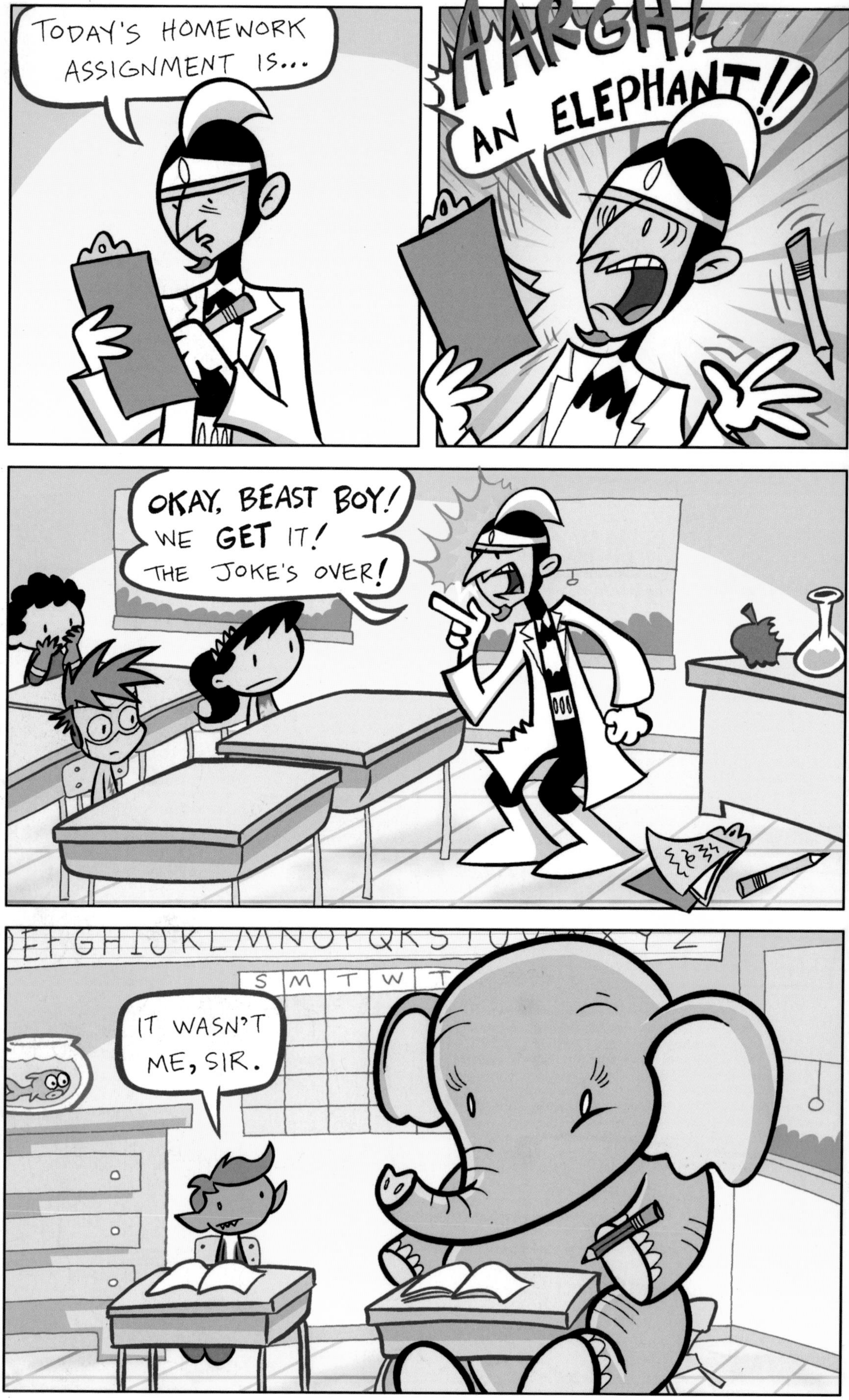
TODAY'S HOMEWORK ASSIGNMENT IS...
AARGH! AN ELEPHANT!!
OKAY, BEAST BOY! WE GET IT! THE JOKE'S OVER!
IT WASN'T ME, SIR.

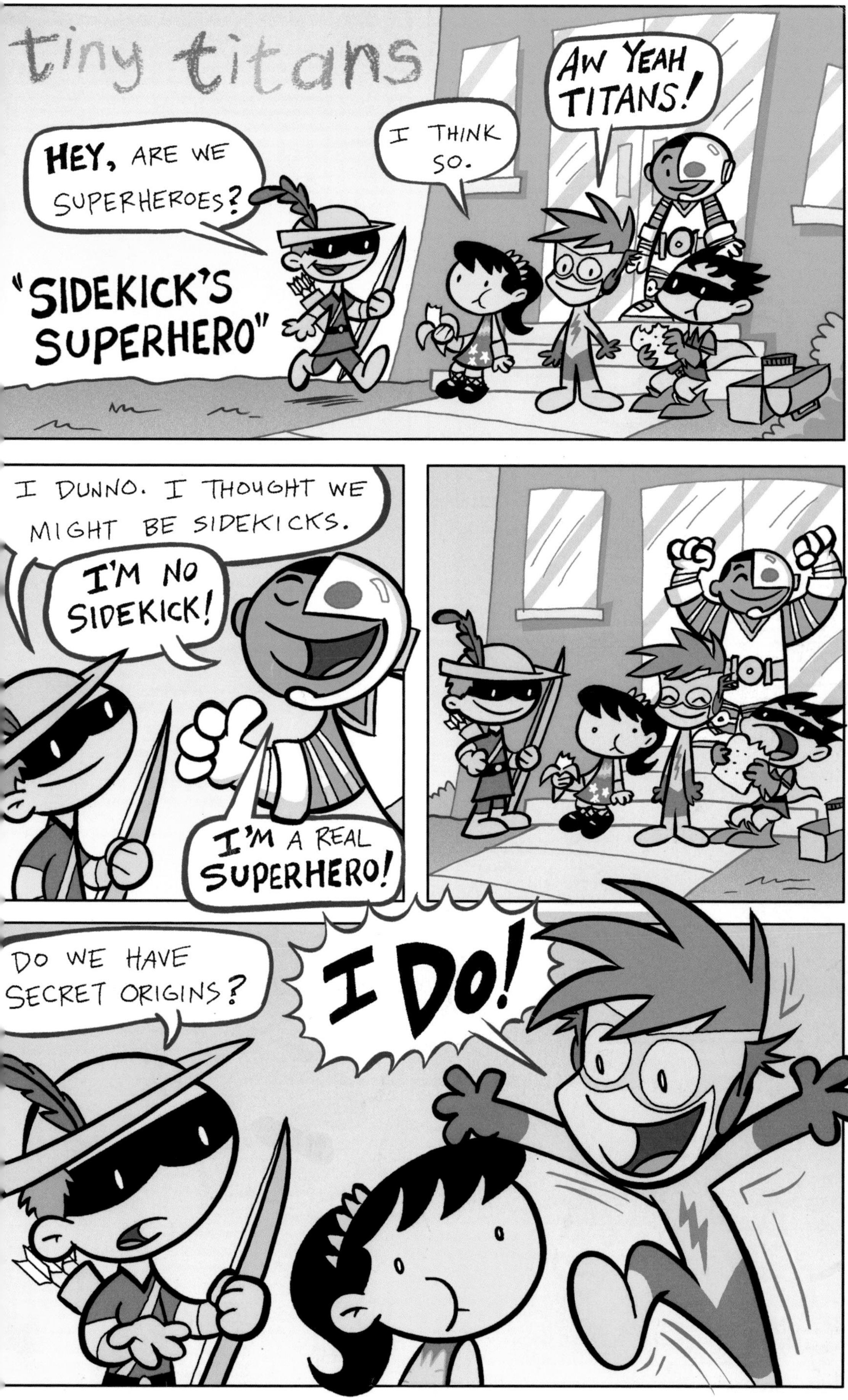
tiny titans
HEY, ARE WE SUPERHEROES?
"SIDEKICK'S SUPERHERO"
I THINK SO.
AW YEAH TITANS!
I DUNNO. I THOUGHT WE MIGHT BE SIDEKICKS.
I'M NO SIDEKICK!
I'M A REAL SUPERHERO!
DO WE HAVE SECRET ORIGINS?
I DO!

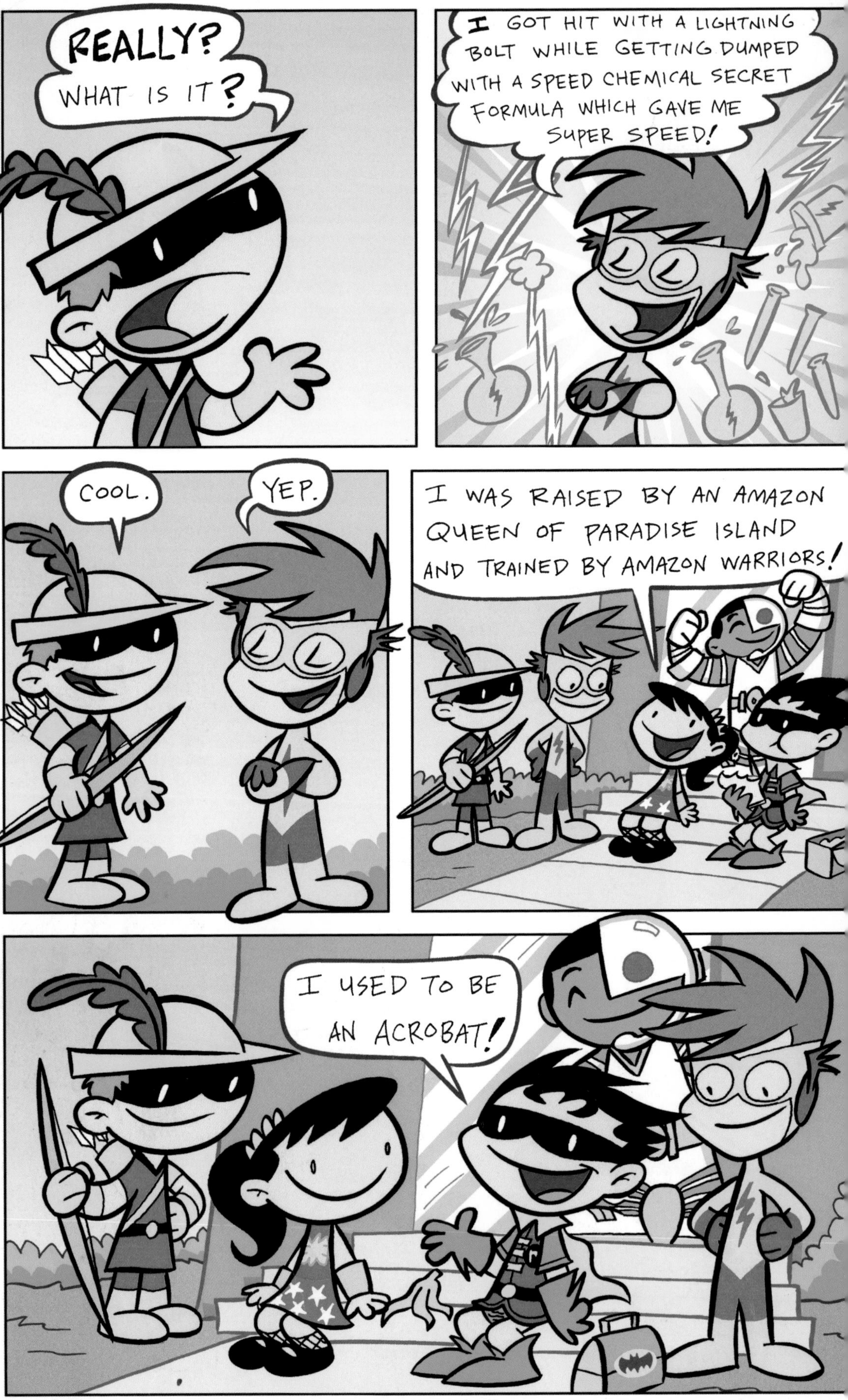
REALLY? WHAT IS IT?
I GOT HIT WITH A LIGHTNING BOLT WHILE GETTING DUMPED WITH A SPEED CHEMICAL SECRET FORMULA WHICH GAVE ME SUPER SPEED!
COOL.
YEP.
I WAS RAISED BY AN AMAZON QUEEN OF PARADISE ISLAND AND TRAINED BY AMAZON WARRIORS!
I USED TO BE AN ACROBAT!

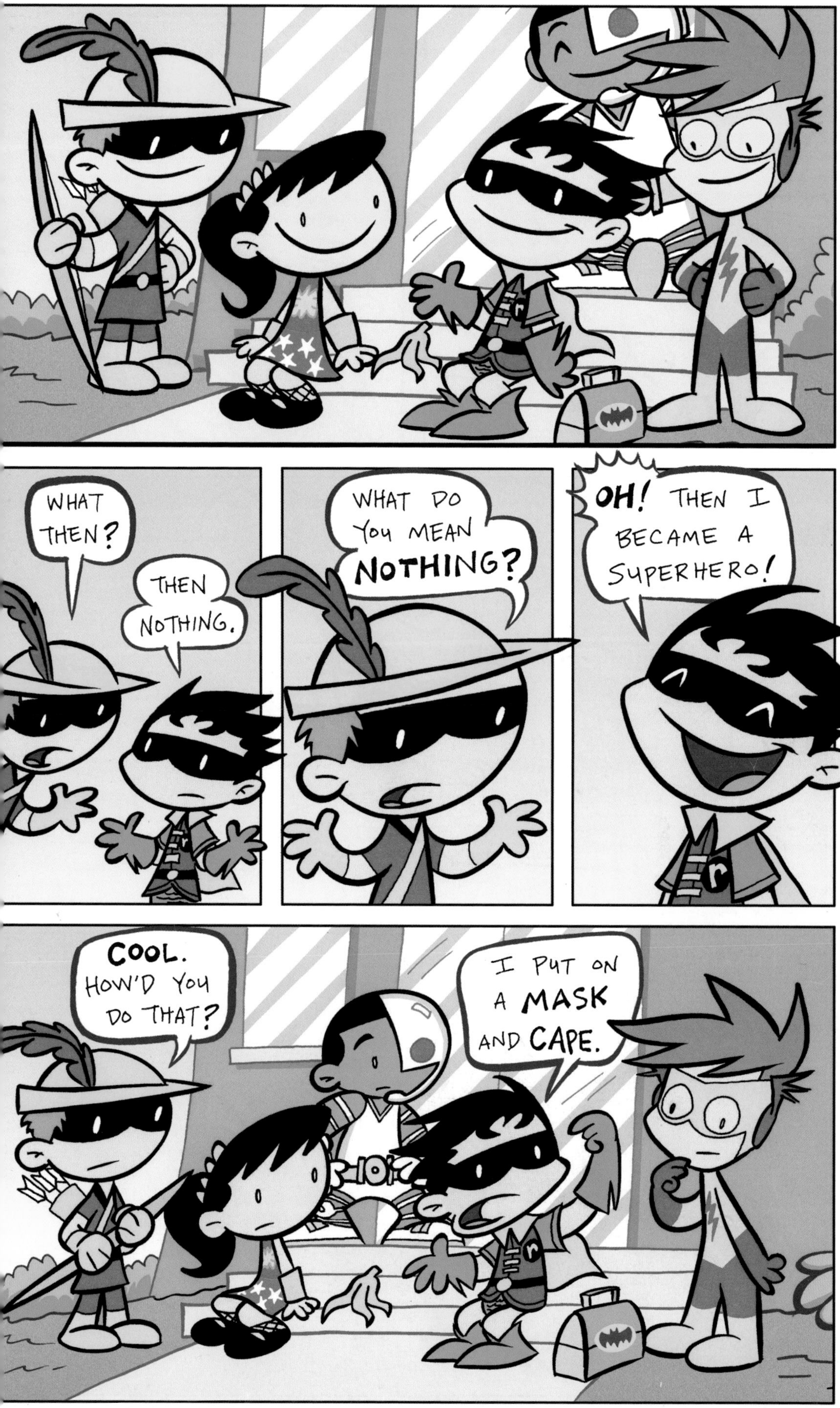

WHAT THEN?
THEN NOTHING.
WHAT DO YOU MEAN NOTHING?
OH! THEN I BECAME A SUPERHERO!
COOL. HOW'D YOU DO THAT?
I PUT ON A MASK AND CAPE.

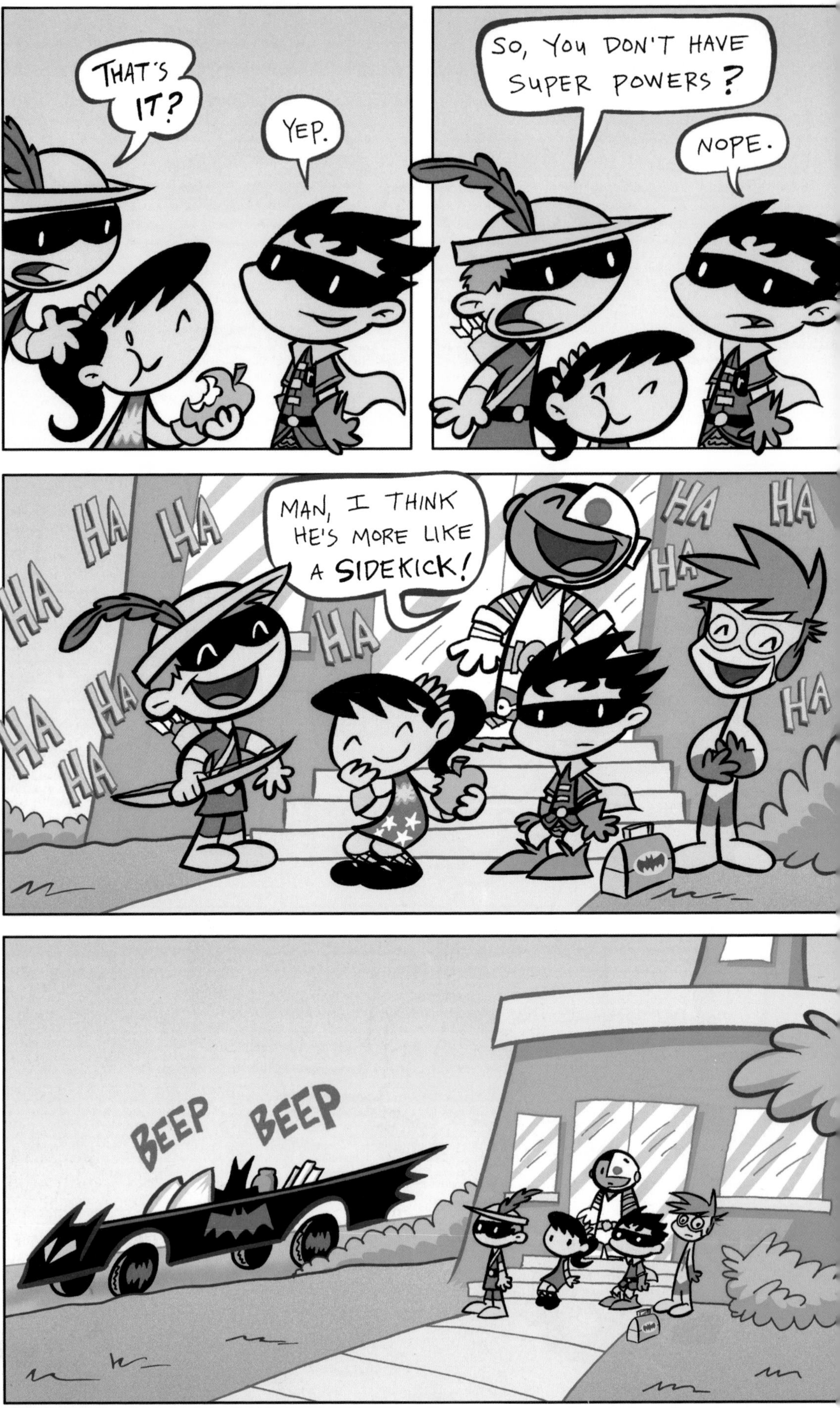
THAT'S IT?
YEP.
SO, YOU DON'T HAVE SUPER POWERS?
NOPE.
HA HA HA HA HA HA HA HA HA HA HA HA
MAN, I THINK HE'S MORE LIKE A SIDEKICK!
BEEP BEEP

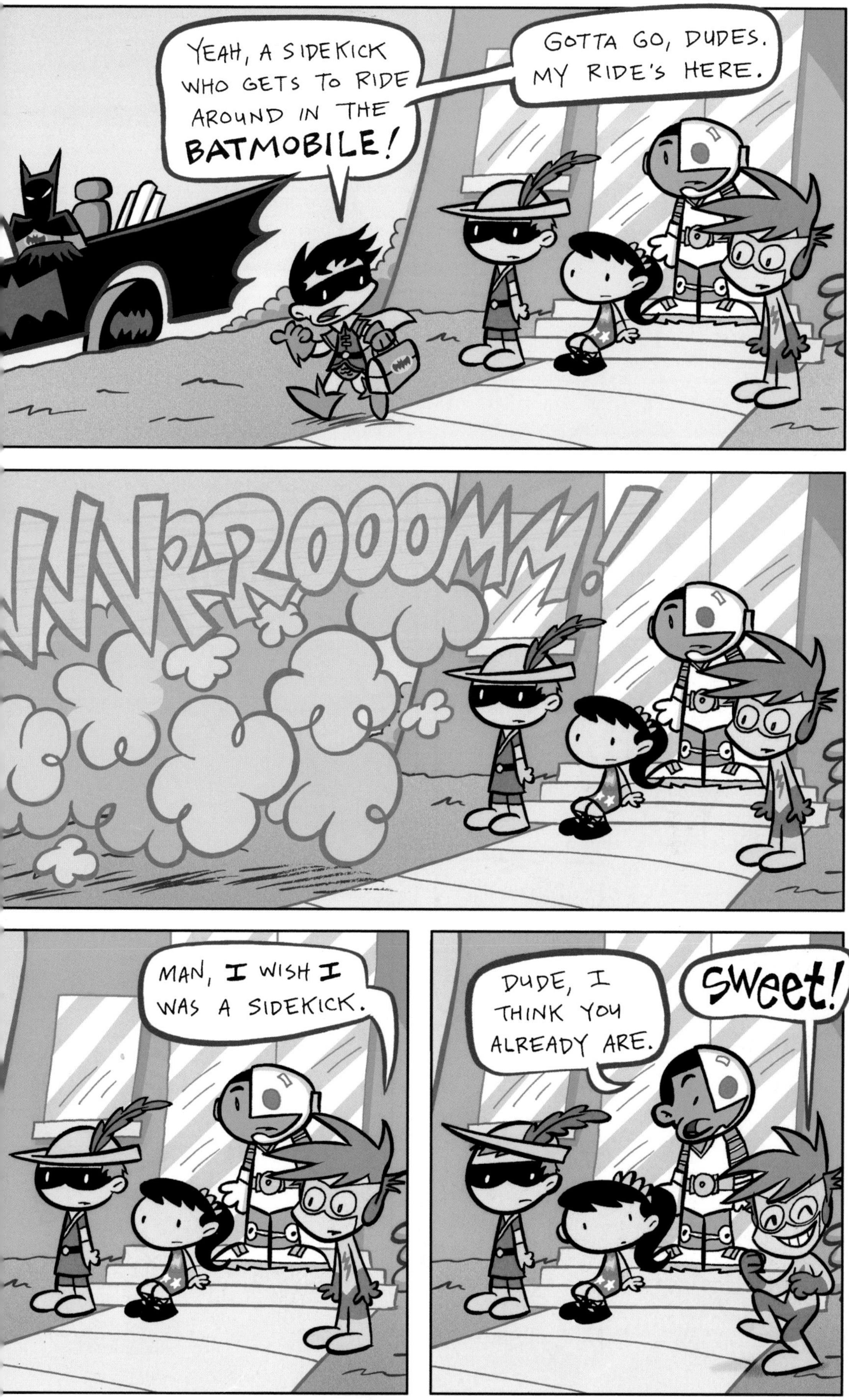
YEAH, A SIDEKICK WHO GETS TO RIDE AROUND IN THE BATMOBILE!
GOTTA GO, DUDES. MY RIDE'S HERE.
VVVRROOOMM!
MAN, I WISH I WAS A SIDEKICK.
DUDE, I THINK YOU ALREADY ARE.
Sweet!

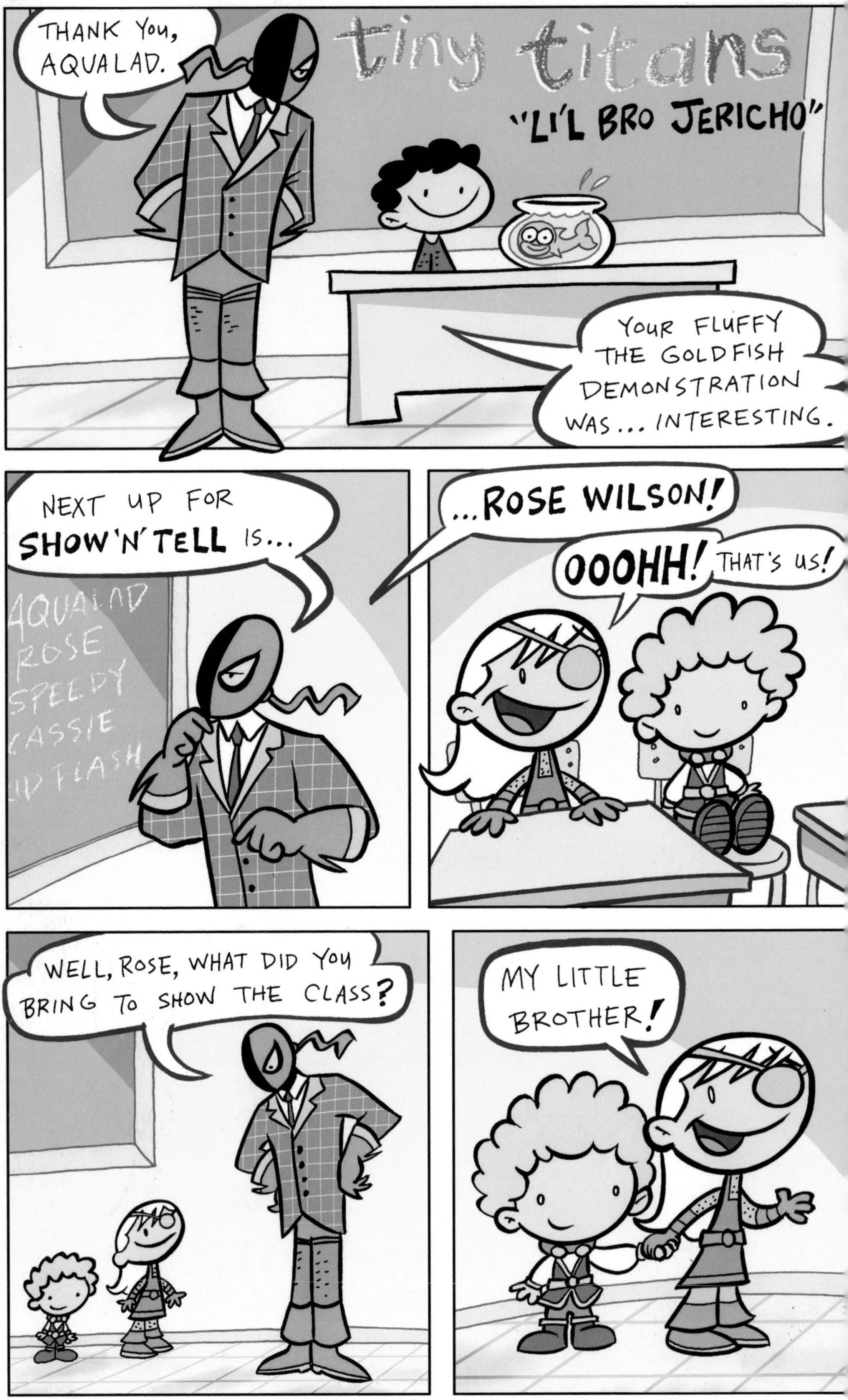

THANK YOU, AQUALAD.
tiny titans
"LI'L BRO JERICHO"
YOUR FLUFFY THE GOLDFISH DEMONSTRATION WAS... INTERESTING.
NEXT UP FOR SHOW'N'TELL IS...
...ROSE WILSON!
OOOHH! THAT'S US!
WELL, ROSE, WHAT DID YOU BRING TO SHOW THE CLASS?
MY LITTLE BROTHER!

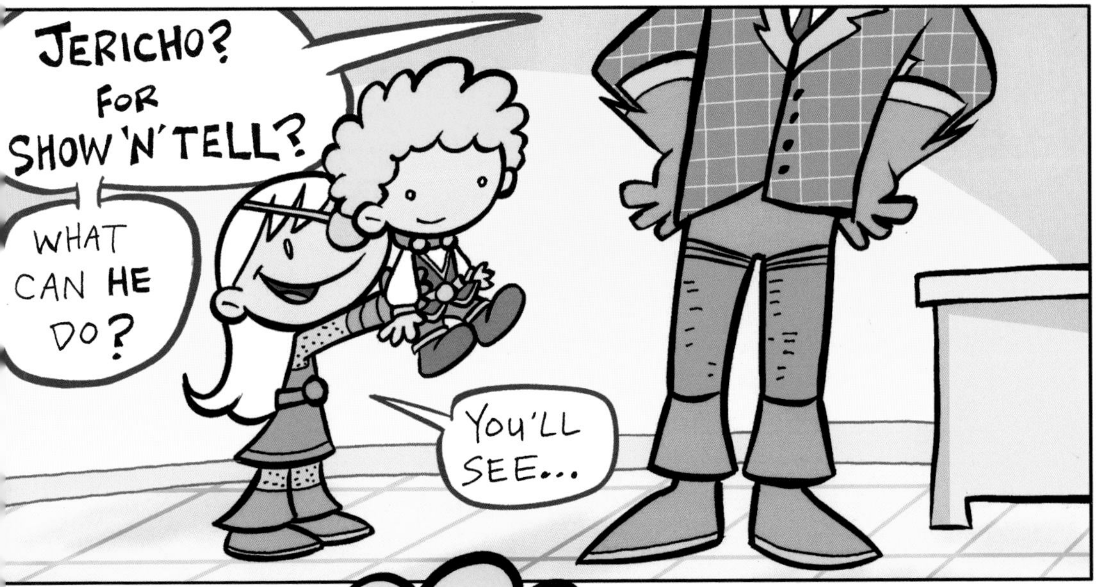
JERICHO? FOR SHOW 'N' TELL?
WHAT CAN HE DO?
YOU'LL SEE...

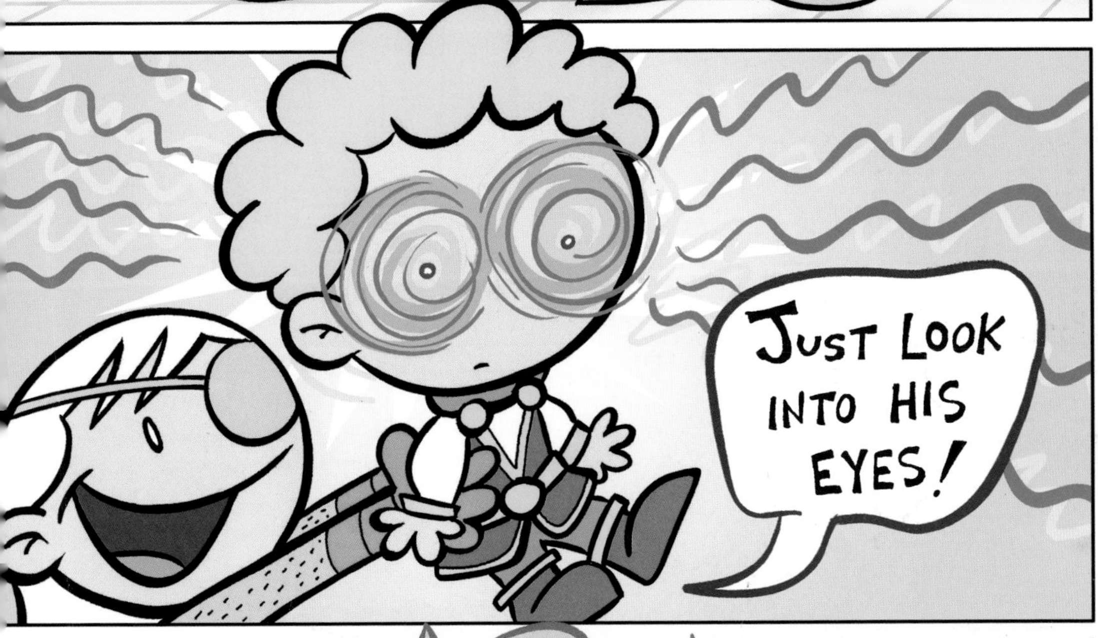
JUST LOOK INTO HIS EYES!

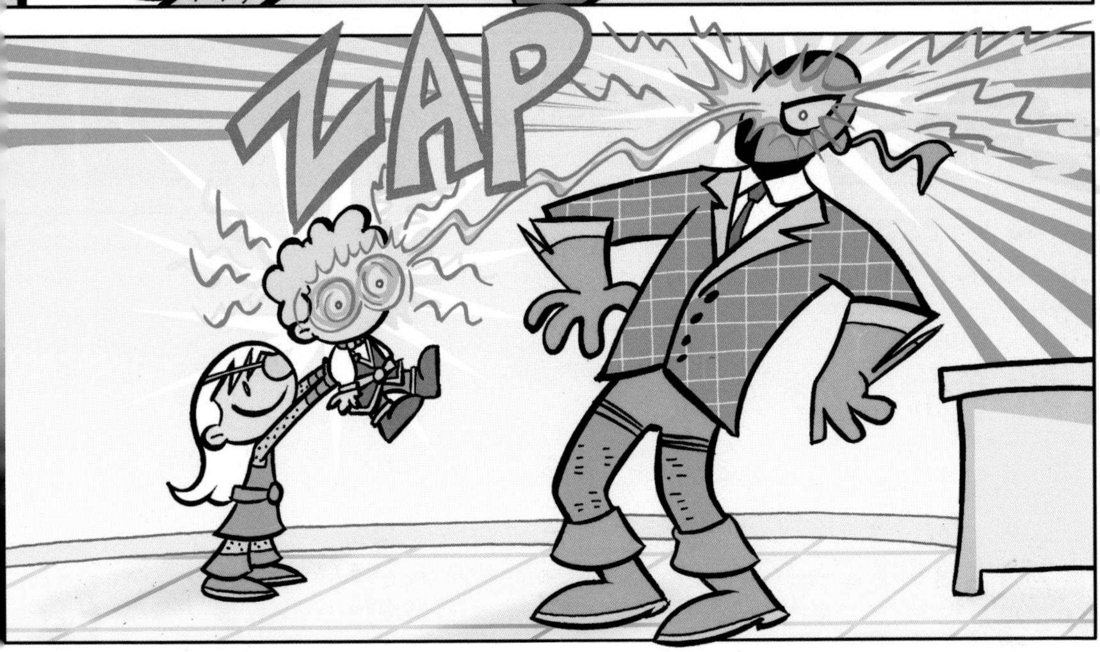
ZAP

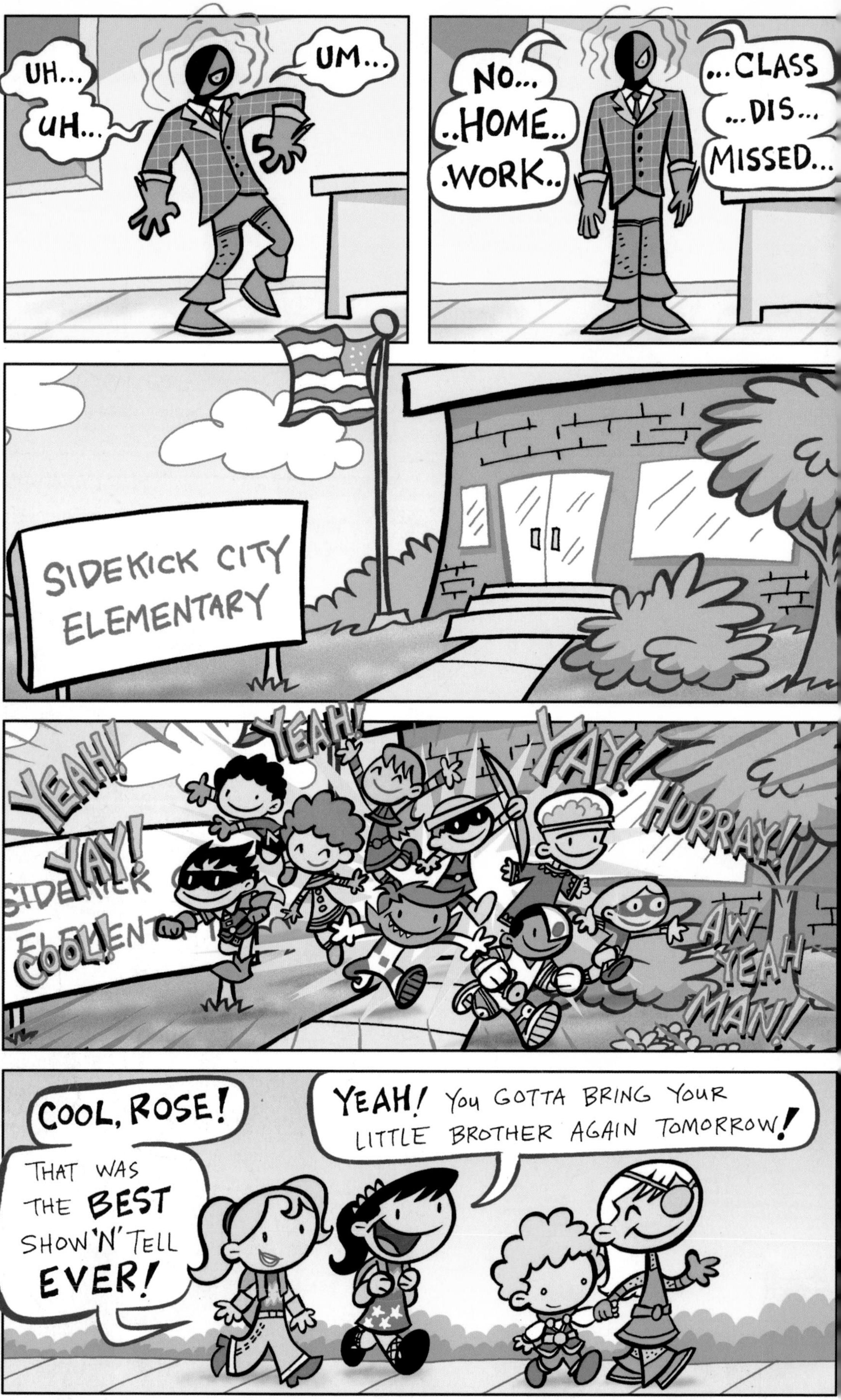
UH...
UH...
UM...
NO...
..HOME..
.WORK..
...CLASS
...DIS...
MISSED...
SIDEKICK CITY
ELEMENTARY
YEAH!
YEAH!
YAY!
YAY!
HURRAY!
COOL!
AW YEAH MAN!
COOL, ROSE!
THAT WAS THE BEST SHOW 'N' TELL EVER!
YEAH! YOU GOTTA BRING YOUR LITTLE BROTHER AGAIN TOMORROW!

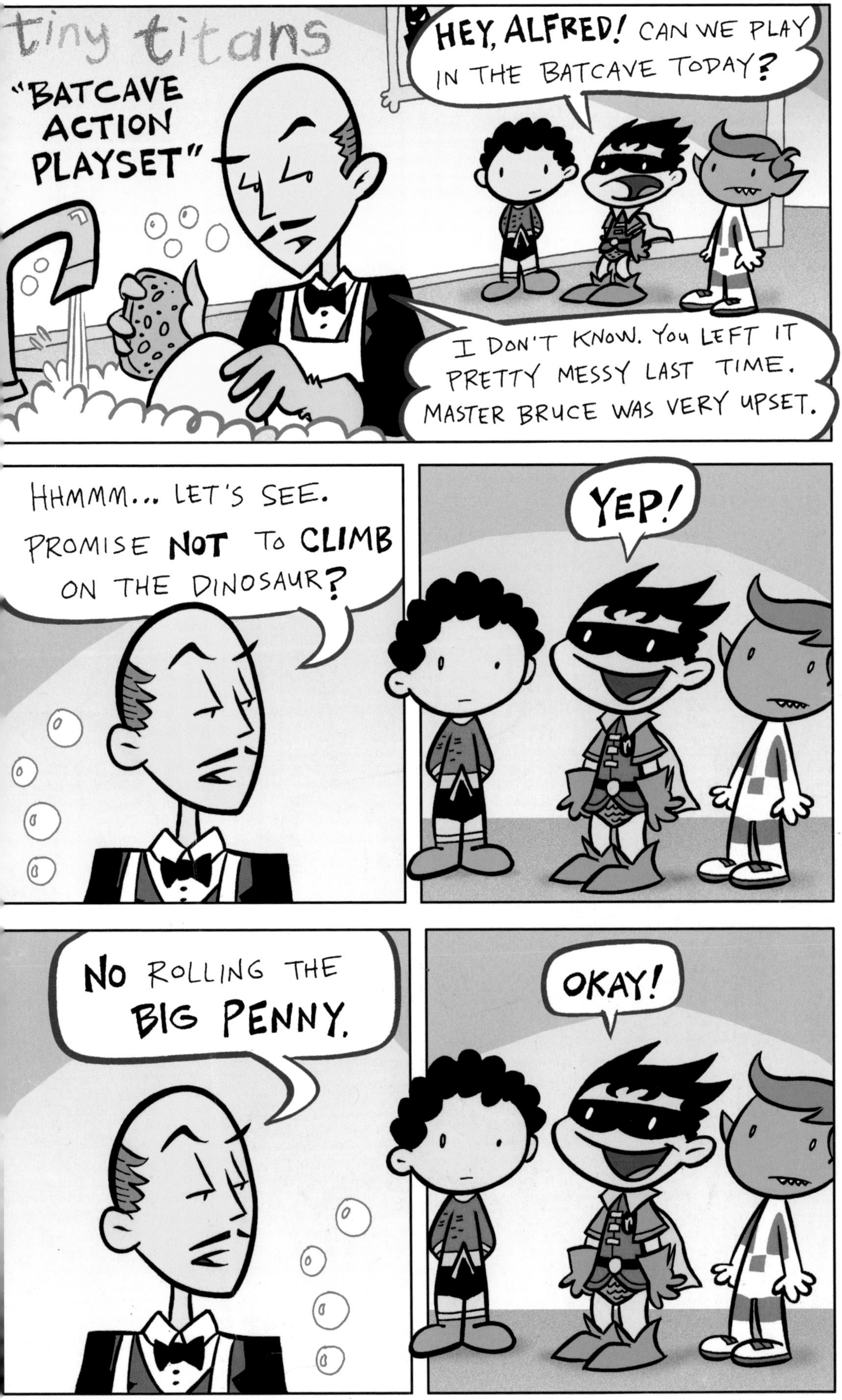

tiny titans
"BATCAVE ACTION PLAYSET"
HEY, ALFRED! CAN WE PLAY IN THE BATCAVE TODAY?
I DON'T KNOW. YOU LEFT IT PRETTY MESSY LAST TIME. MASTER BRUCE WAS VERY UPSET.
HHMMM... LET'S SEE. PROMISE NOT TO CLIMB ON THE DINOSAUR?
YEP!
NO ROLLING THE BIG PENNY.
OKAY!

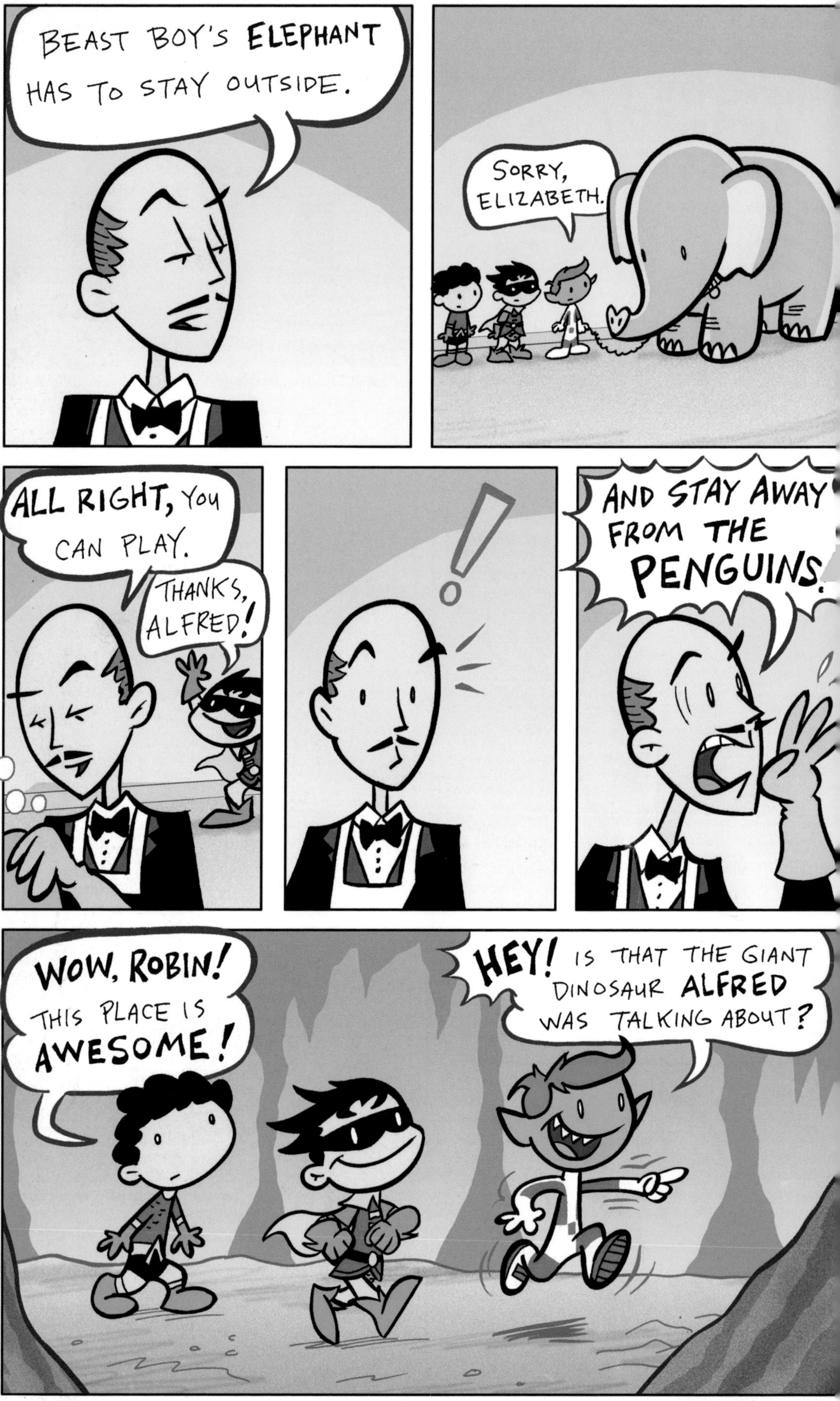

BEAST BOY'S ELEPHANT HAS TO STAY OUTSIDE.
SORRY, ELIZABETH.
ALL RIGHT, YOU CAN PLAY.
THANKS, ALFRED!
!
AND STAY AWAY FROM THE PENGUINS!
WOW, ROBIN! THIS PLACE IS AWESOME!
HEY! IS THAT THE GIANT DINOSAUR ALFRED WAS TALKING ABOUT?

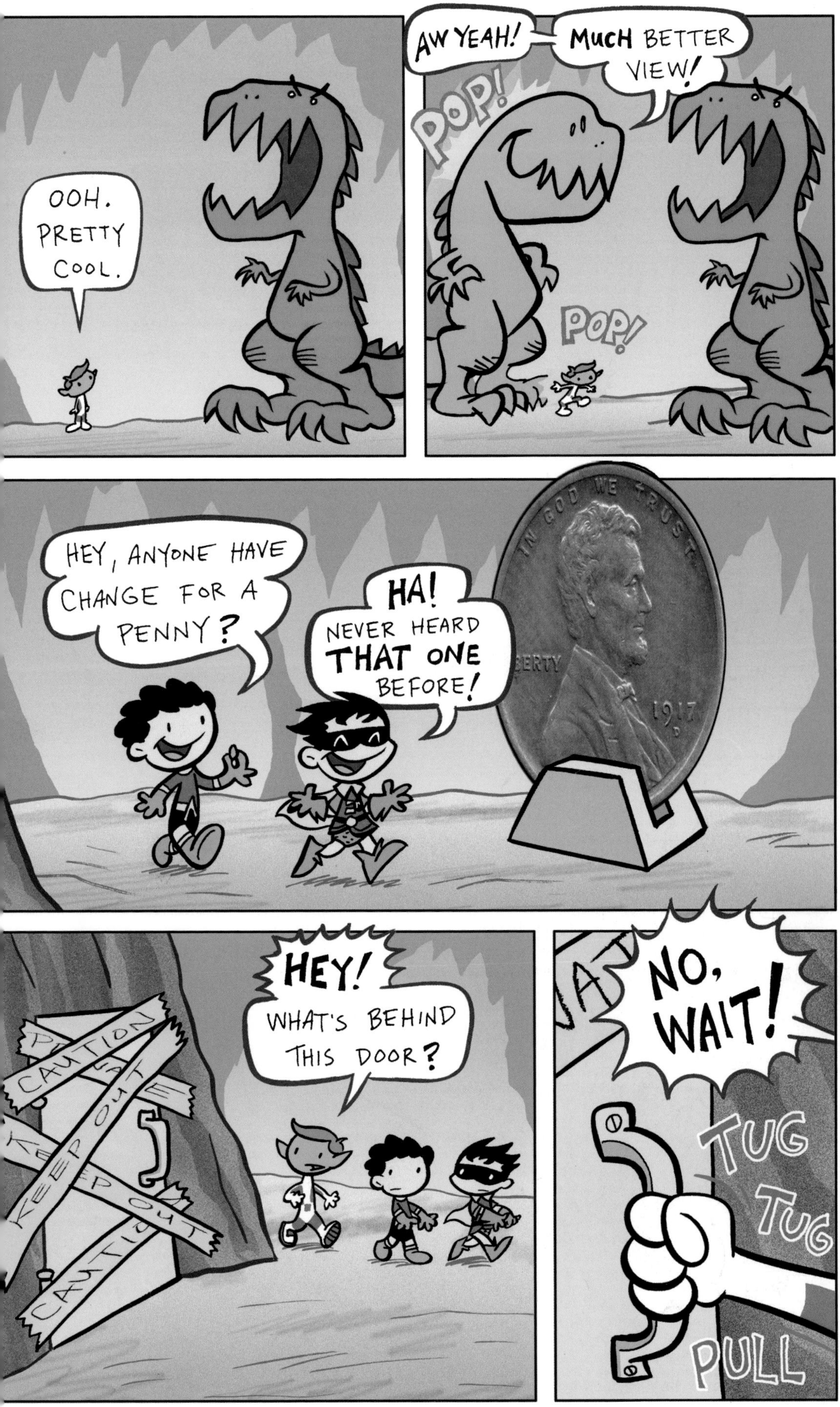
OOH. PRETTY COOL.
AW YEAH!
MUCH BETTER VIEW!
POP!
POP!
HEY, ANYONE HAVE CHANGE FOR A PENNY?
HA! NEVER HEARD THAT ONE BEFORE!
IN GOD WE TRUST
1917
HEY! WHAT'S BEHIND THIS DOOR?
CAUTION
KEEP OUT
KEEP OUT
CAUTION
NO, WAIT!
TUG
TUG
PULL

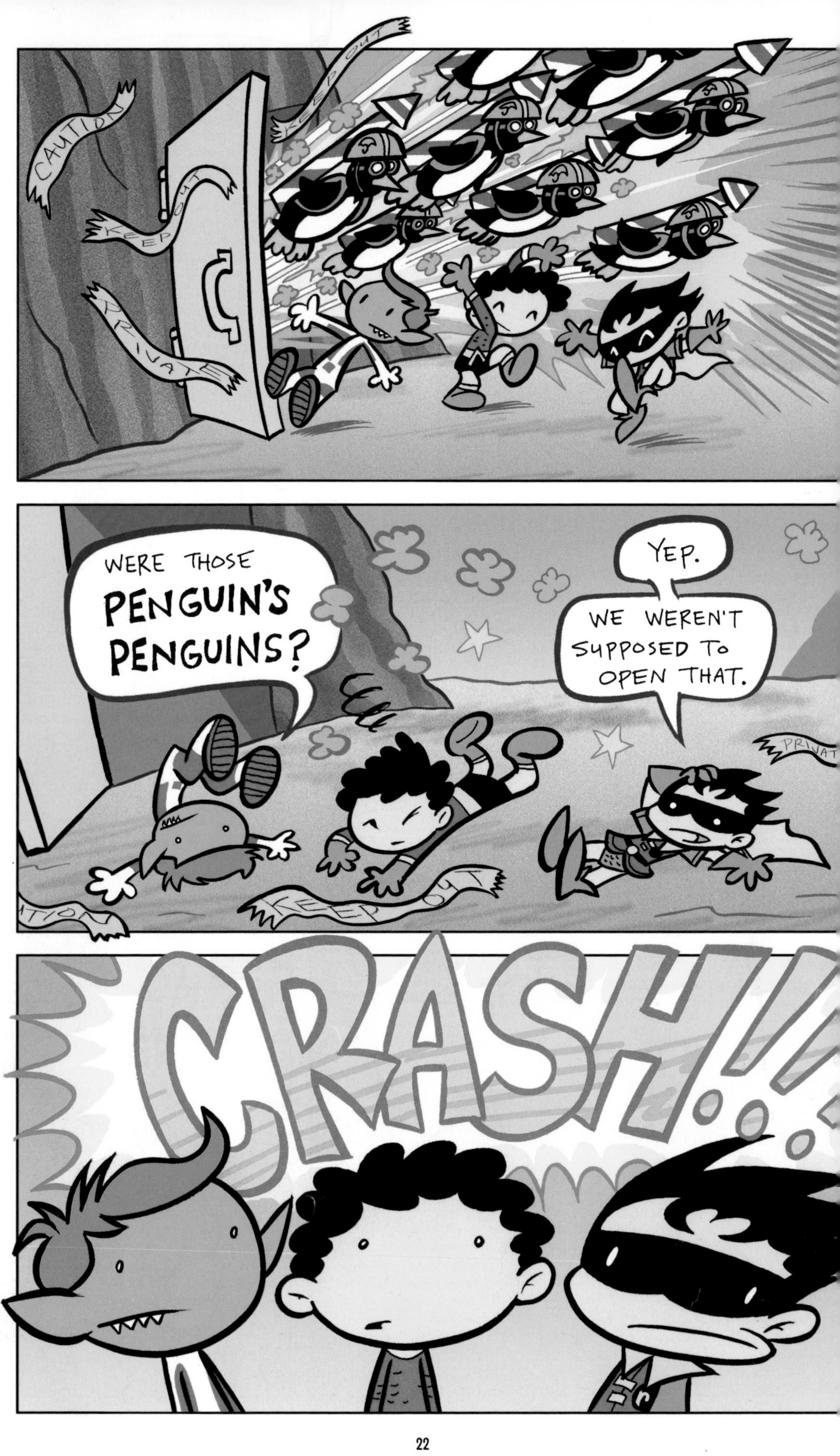
KEEP OUT
CAUTION
KEEP OUT
PRIVATE
WERE THOSE PENGUIN'S PENGUINS?
YEP.
WE WEREN'T SUPPOSED TO OPEN THAT.
KEEP OUT
CRASH!!

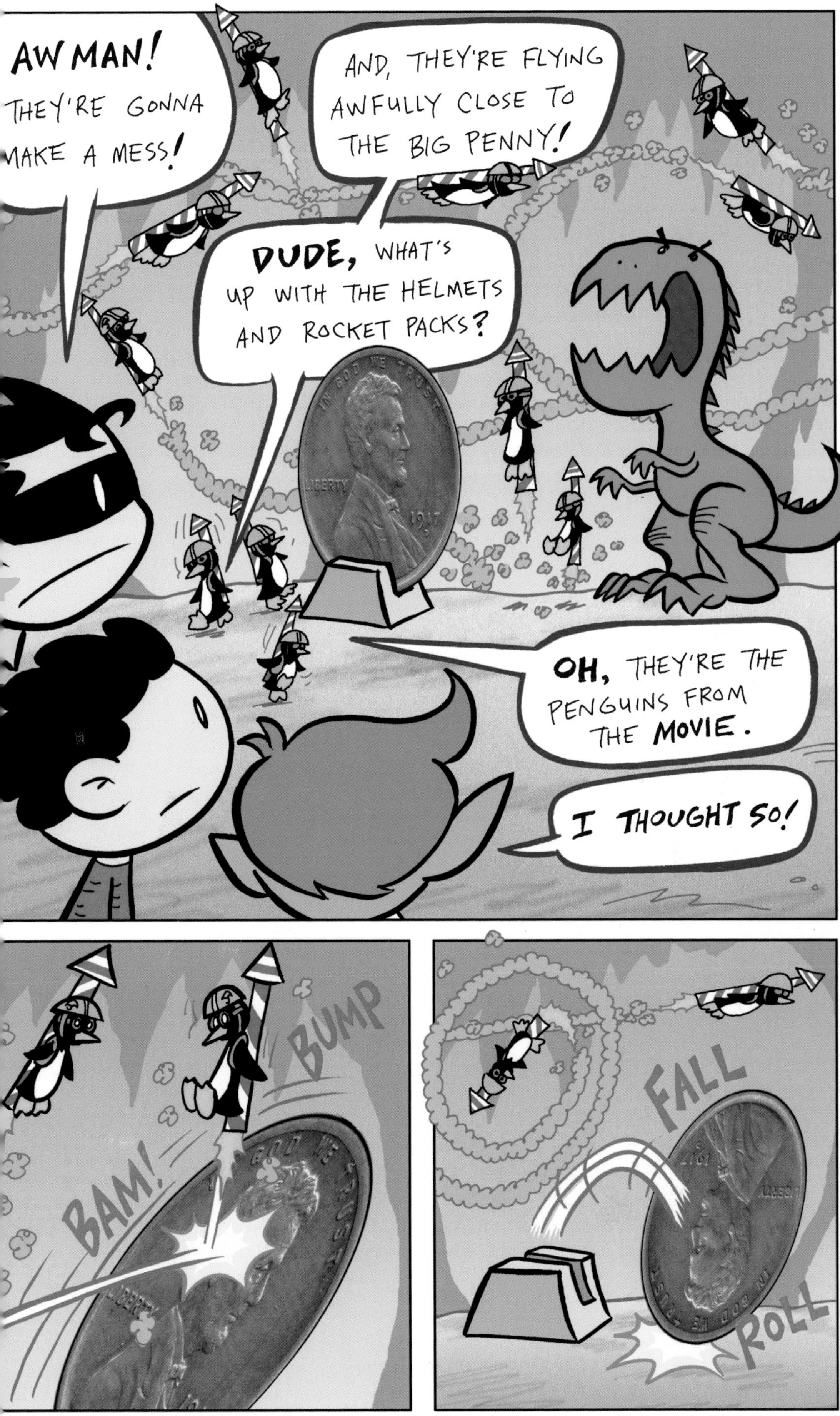

AW MAN! THEY'RE GONNA MAKE A MESS!
AND, THEY'RE FLYING AWFULLY CLOSE TO THE BIG PENNY!
DUDE, WHAT'S UP WITH THE HELMETS AND ROCKET PACKS?
OH, THEY'RE THE PENGUINS FROM THE MOVIE.
I THOUGHT SO!
BUMP
BAM!
FALL
ROLL

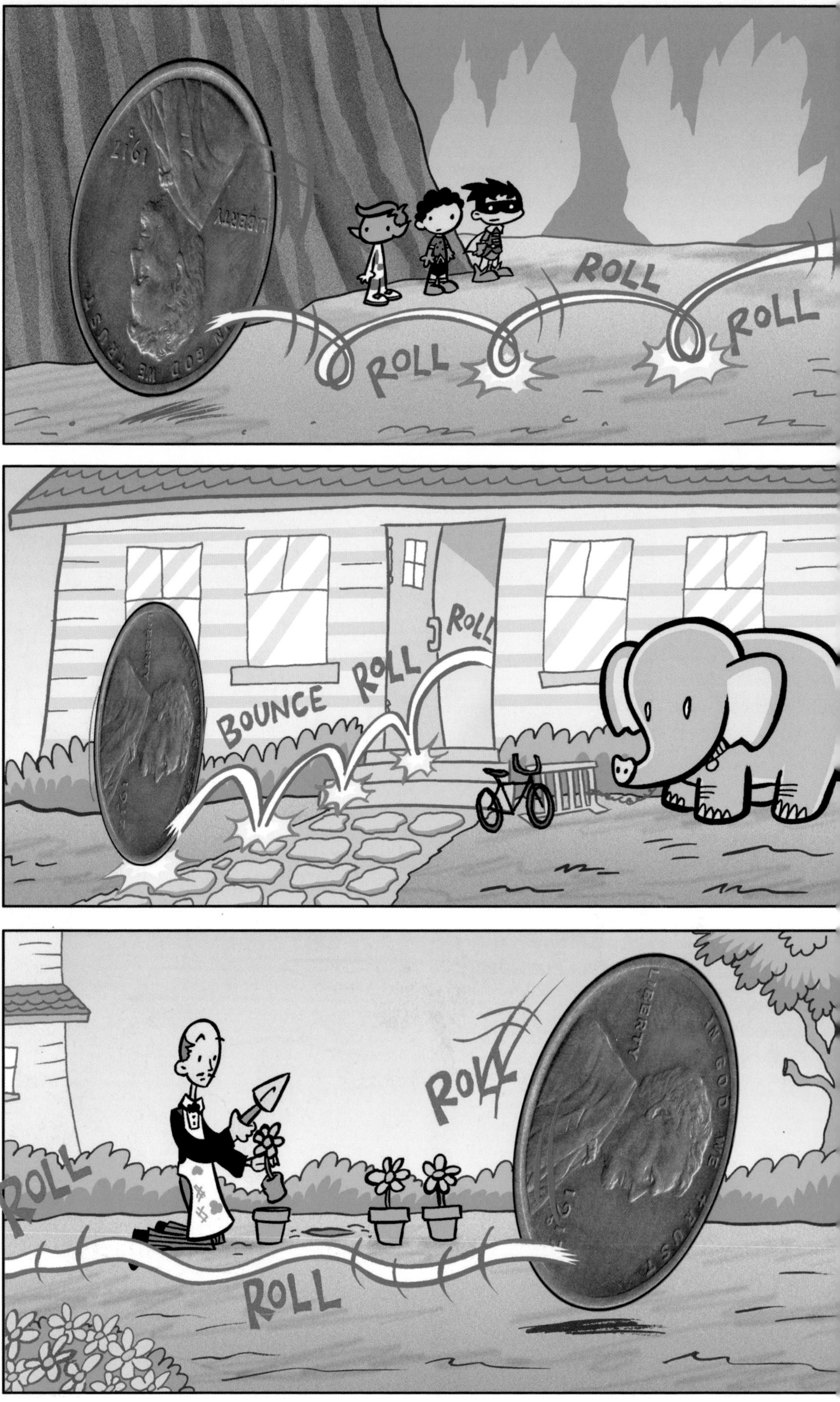
ROLL
ROLL
ROLL
BOUNCE
ROLL
ROLL
ROLL
ROLL
ROLL

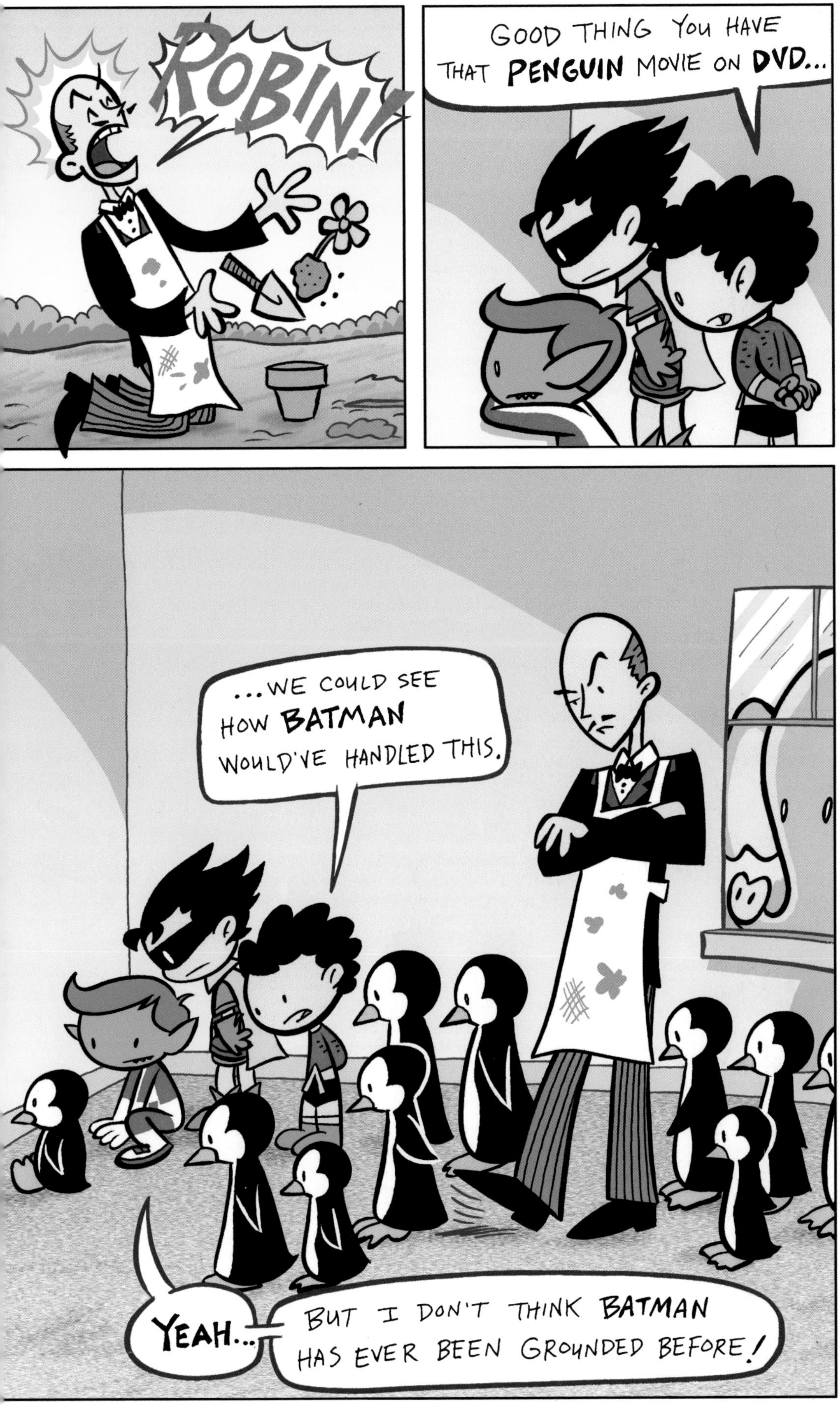
ROBIN!
GOOD THING YOU HAVE THAT PENGUIN MOVIE ON DVD...
...WE COULD SEE HOW BATMAN WOULD'VE HANDLED THIS.
YEAH...
BUT I DON'T THINK BATMAN HAS EVER BEEN GROUNDED BEFORE!

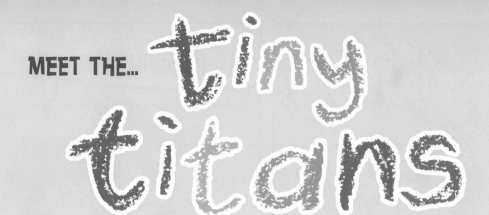

MEET THE... tiny titans

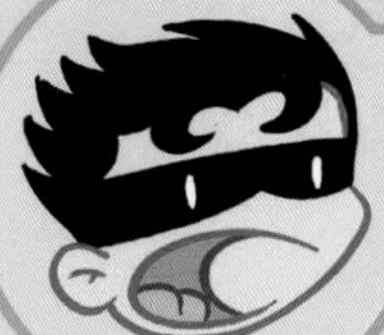

ROBIN

(Dick Grayson)- The brave and serious leader of the Tiny Titans. Although he is the original Robin, he is very moody and has to share his room with his brothers, the other Robins. Also, he has secret crushes for Starfire and Barbara Gordon.

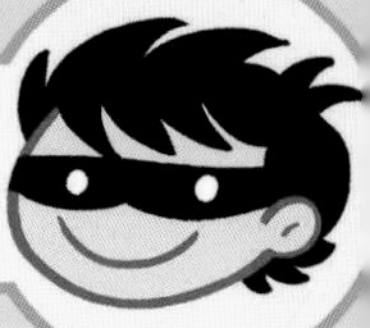

JASON TODDLER

The youngest of the three Robins. Too young to go to school, Jason is always in a happy mood and has a care-free style. He's all about smiling and having fun.

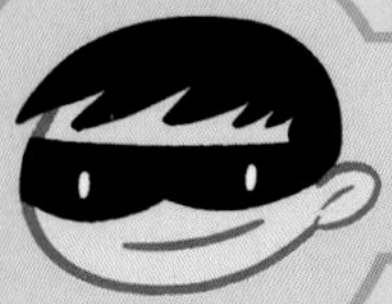

TIM DRAKE

The cool Robin. Tim wants to stand out from his brothers by wearing his own unique Robin costume. He's very laid back and easy going indeed.

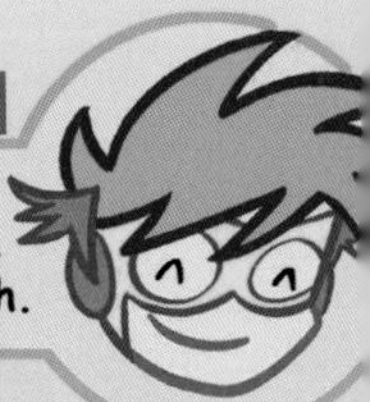

KID FLASH

The super speedster and fasted kid in the school. Quick witted and eats lots for lunch because of his high metabolism. Too much candy will cause major sugar rush.

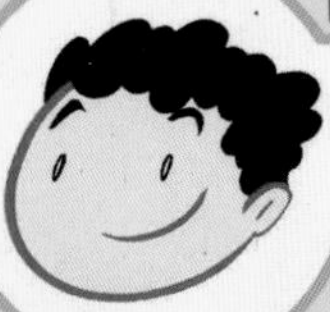

AQUALAD

The little boy from the ocean. Has a pet fish named Fluffy. Aqualad can communicate with all forms of sea life, even the pet hamster in their classroom.

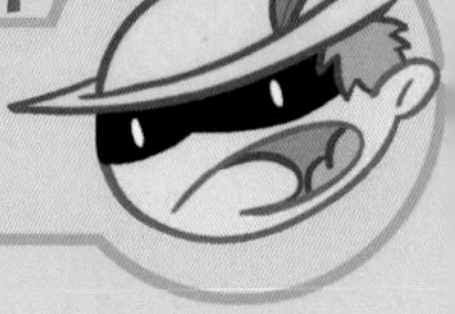

SPEEDY

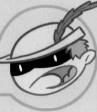

Quiet and cool, he is the boy with the trick arrows. He's good at anything that requires aiming. Also, he's Kid Flash's best friend.

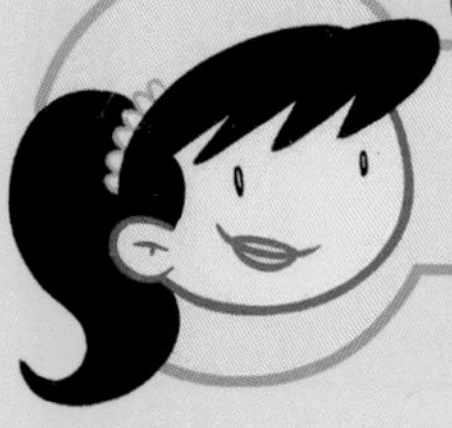

WONDER GIRL

(Donna) Raised by amazons. She's strong and cute. Never lie to her, she has a magical jump rope which makes people tell the truth. Very skeptic.

RAVEN

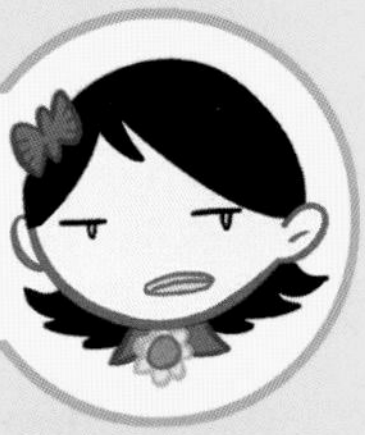

The quiet and mysterious little girl. She really likes to experiment with dark magic, which usually turn into bad practical jokes. Mr. Trigon, the substitute teacher is her father.

CYBORG

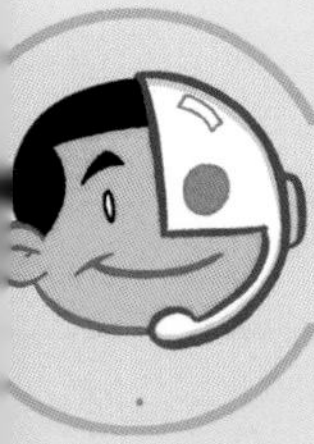

Half boy, half robot. Cyborg is always tinkering with mechanical gadgets, often turning them into something else. His battle cry "BOO-YA!" has earned him the nickname, "Big Boo-Ya".

BEAST BOY

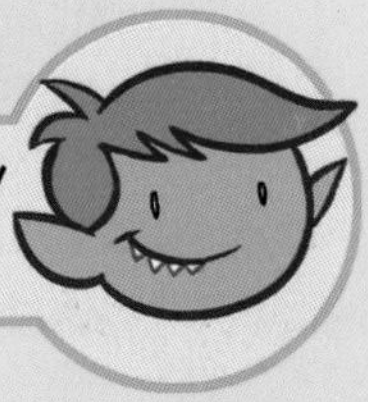

The green little boy who can change into any animal he desires. He's a prankster and loves comics. Has a crush on Terra.

STARFIRE

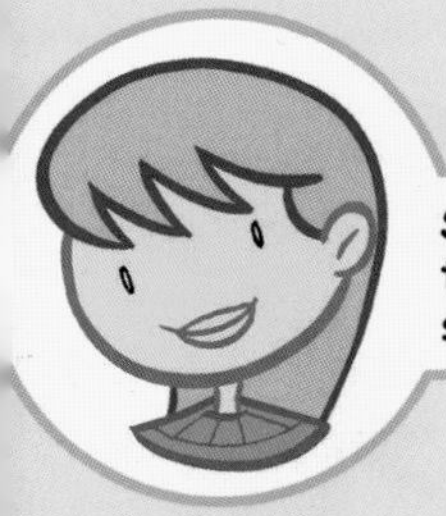

She's an alien princess. Very naïve and free spirited and finds the good in others. Has a crush on Robin and thinks he's cute, but so do all the other girls.

KID DEVIL

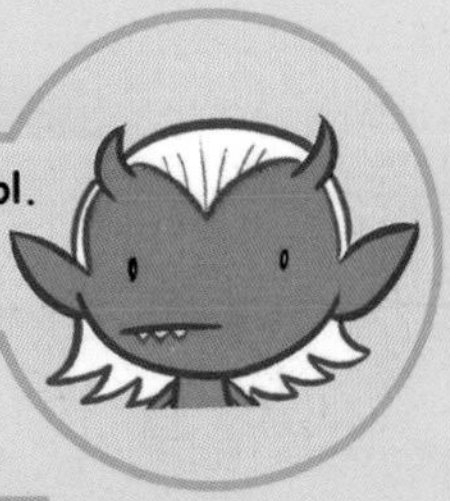

One of the younger Tiny Titans, still too young for school. Cannot talk but can breathe fire, usually while coughing or sneezing or hiccupping.

ROSE & JERICHO

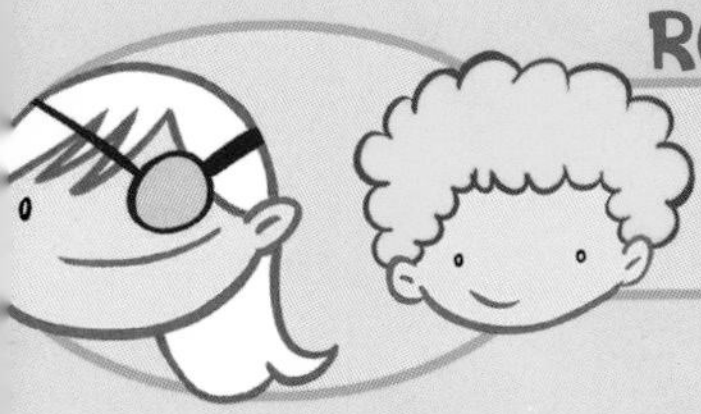

Principal Slade's kids. Rose is the older and tougher "Tom-Boy" of the two. Jericho can't speak, but can take over your mind if you look into his eyes.

MISS MARTIAN

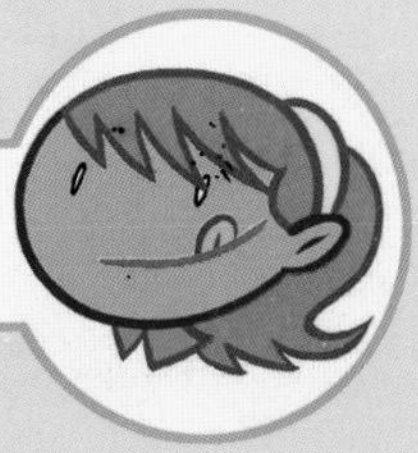

A shape shifting little girl alien from Mars who is still too young to go to school. She is often mistaken for Beast Boy's little sister.

TERRA

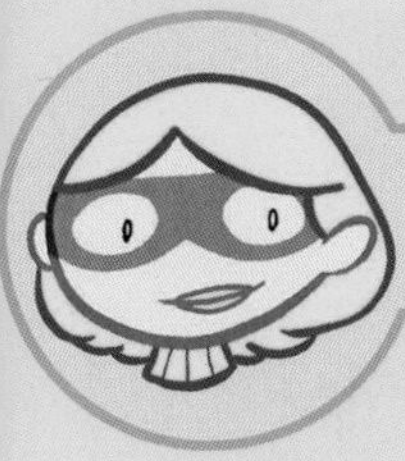

The sometimes hated little girl who likes to throw rocks. Principal Slade's teacher's pet. She thinks Beast Boy is a weirdo.

CASSIE

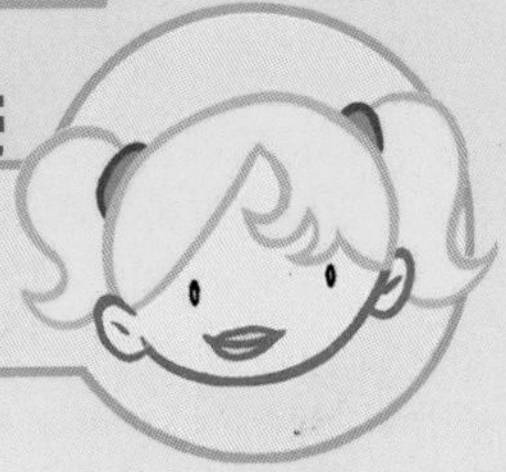

Wonder Girl's rich cousin from the big city. Cassie's really into fashion and is hip to all the latest trends in POP culture.

BUMBLE BEE

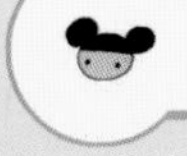

The tiniest of the Tiny Titans.
BB buzzes and packs a mighty stinger.

Creators

Art Baltazar is a cartoonist machine from the heart of Chicago! He defines cartoons and comics not only as an art style, but as a way of life. Currently, Art is the creative force behind *The New York Times* best-selling, Eisner Award-winning, DC Comics series Tiny Titans, and the co-writer for Billy Batson and the Magic of SHAZAM! and co-creator of Superman Family Adventures. Art is living the dream! He draws comics and never has to leave the house. He lives with his lovely wife, Rose, big boy Sonny, little boy Gordon, and little girl Audrey. Right on!

ART BALTAZAR

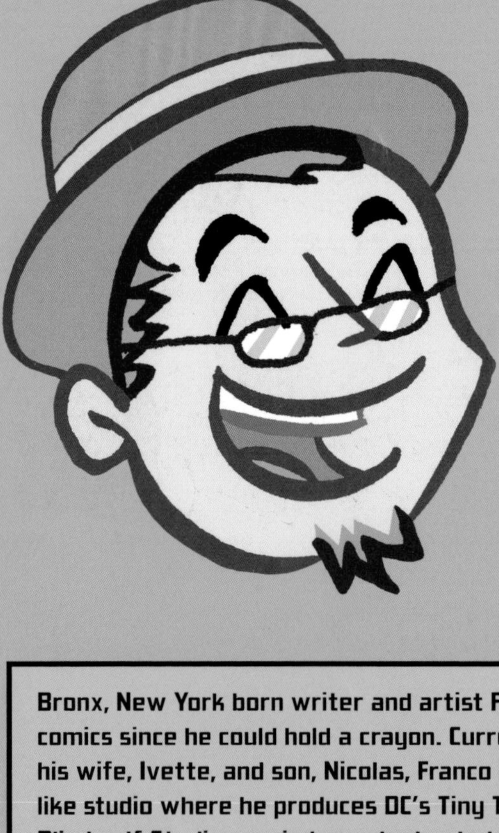

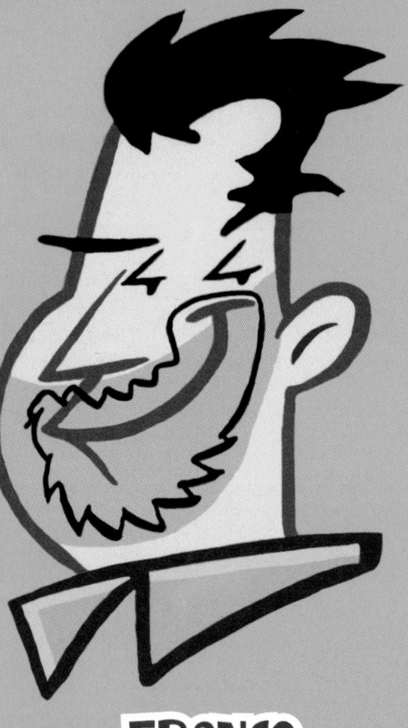

FRANCO

Bronx, New York born writer and artist Franco Aureliani has been drawing comics since he could hold a crayon. Currently residing in upstate New York with his wife, Ivette, and son, Nicolas, Franco spends most of his days in a Batcave-like studio where he produces DC's Tiny Titans comics. In 1995, Franco founded Blindwolf Studios, an independent art studio where he and fellow creators can create children's comics. Franco is the creator, artist, and writer of Weirdsville, L'il Creeps, and Eagle All Star, as well as the co-creator and writer of Patrick the Wolf Boy. When he's not writing and drawing, Franco also teaches high school art.

Glossary

ACROBAT [AK-ruh-bat] - a person who performs exciting gymnastic acts that require great skill; acrobats often work with a circus.

ASSIGNMENT [uh-SINE-muhnt] - a specific job that is given to somebody

CHEMICAL [KEM-uh-kuhl] - a substance used in chemistry

DEMONSTRATION [dem-uhn-STREY-shuhn] - a description or explanation illustrated by examples

EXPERIMENT [ek-SPIHR-uh-ment] - a scientific test to try out a theory or to see the effect of something

FORMULA [FOR-myuh-luh] - a rule in science or math that is written with numbers and symbols

ORIGIN [OR-uh-jin] - the point where something began

Action Accessories

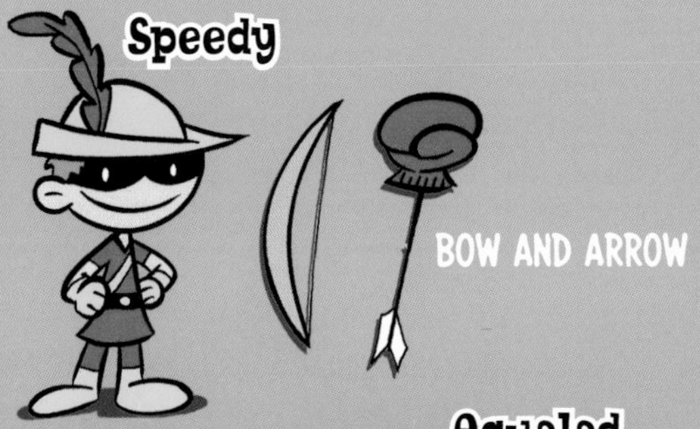
Speedy
BOW AND ARROW

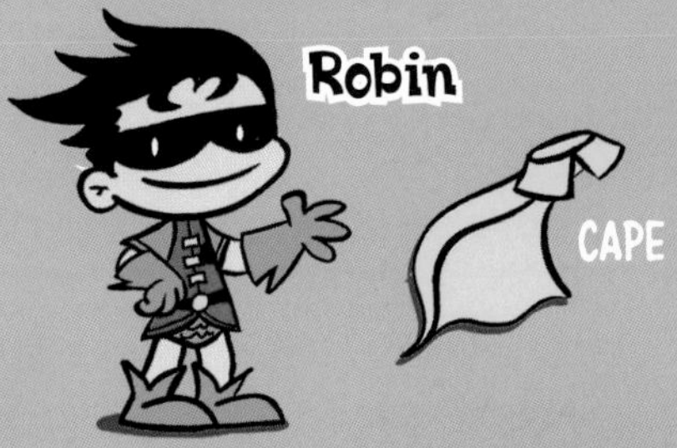
Robin
CAPE

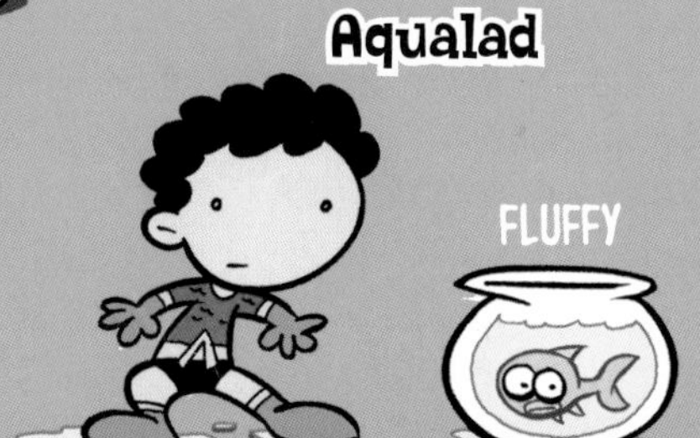
Aqualad
FLUFFY

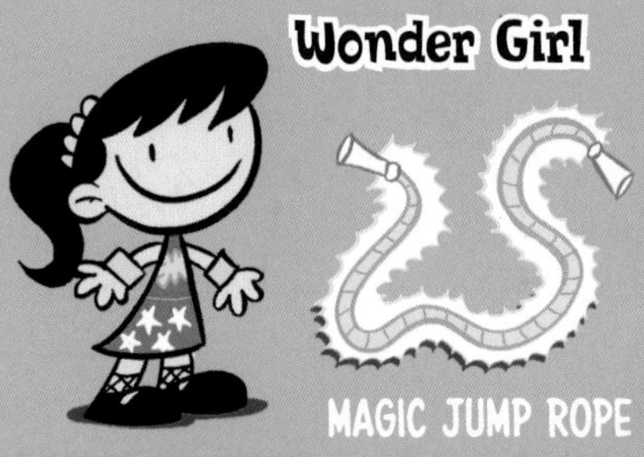
Wonder Girl
MAGIC JUMP ROPE

Visual Questions & Prompt

1. WHAT DO THE SOUND EFFECTS IN THE FOLLOWING PANEL TELL YOU ABOUT WHAT'S HAPPENING IN THE STORY? TALK ABOUT THE SEQUENCE OF EVENTS.

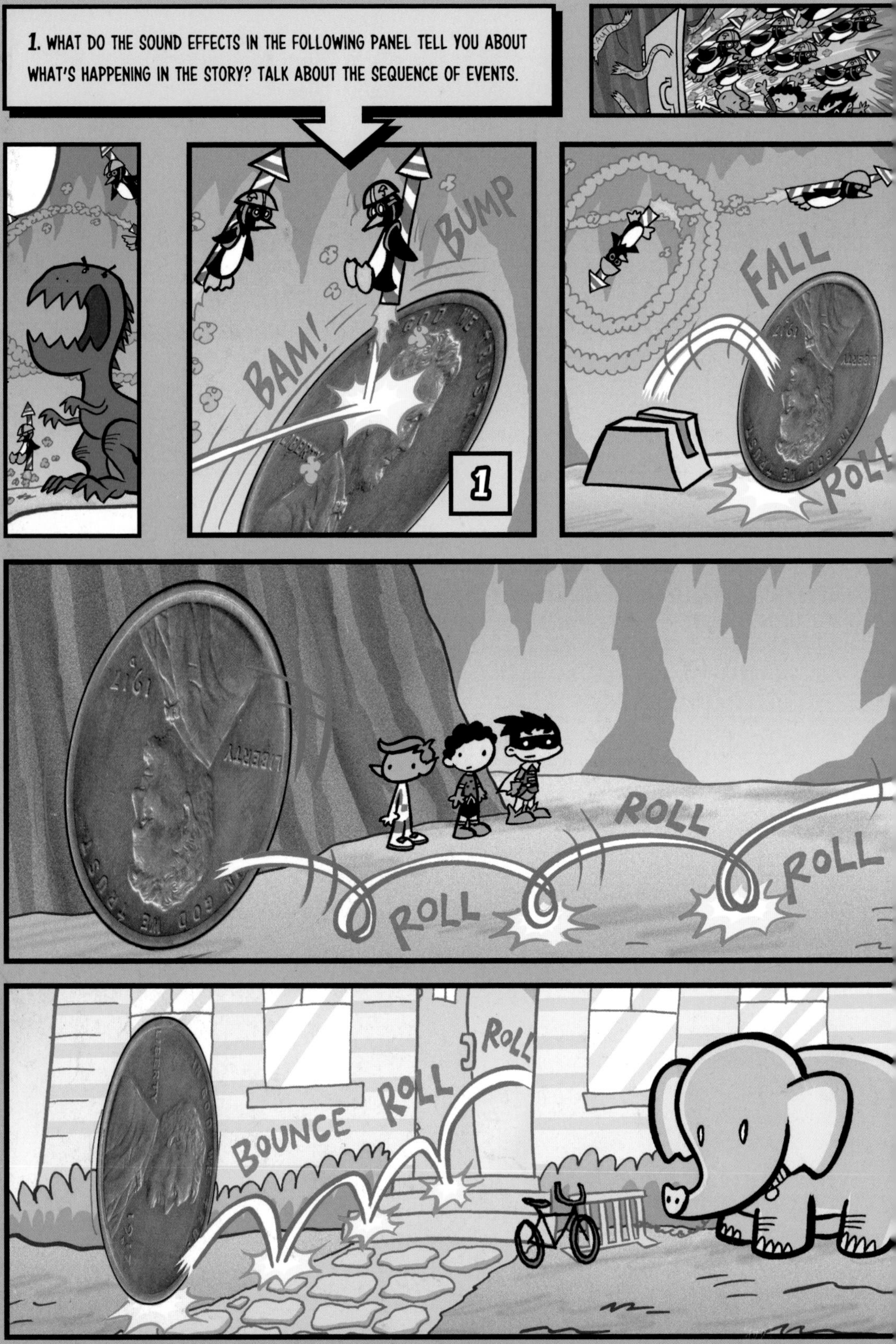

BUMP
BAM!
1
FALL
ROLL
ROLL
ROLL
ROLL
BOUNCE
ROLL
ROLL

2. WHAT ARE THE DIFFERENT ANIMALS BEAST BOY CHANGES INTO? IF YOU HAD HIS SUPERPOWER AND COULD CHANGE INTO SOMETHING ELSE, WHAT YOU WOULD PICK? TALK ABOUT WHAT YOU WOULD CHOOSE, AND WHY.

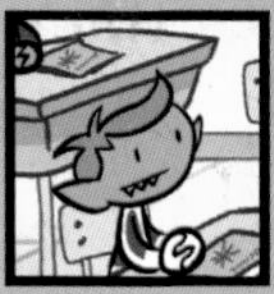

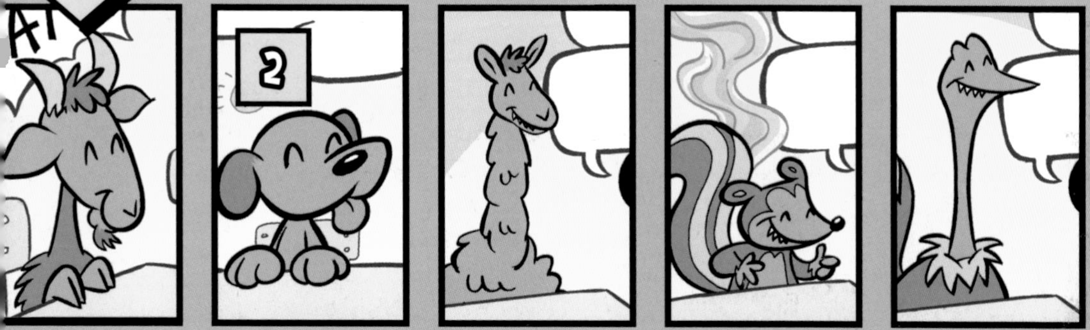
2

3. WHAT DID JERICHO DO THAT MADE THE OTHER STUDENTS DECIDE HE WAS THE BEST SHOW 'N' TELL EVER? EXPLAIN.

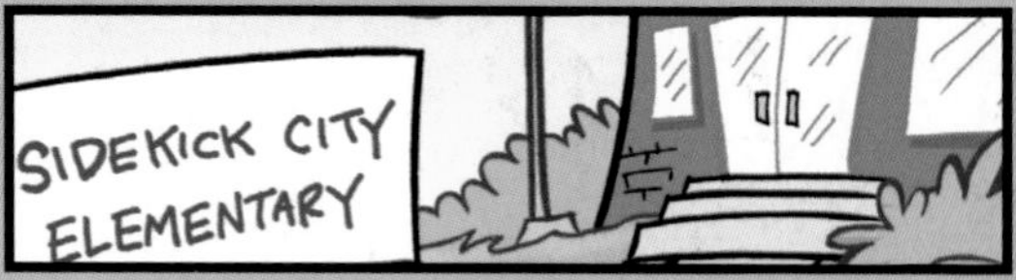
SIDEKICK CITY
ELEMENTARY

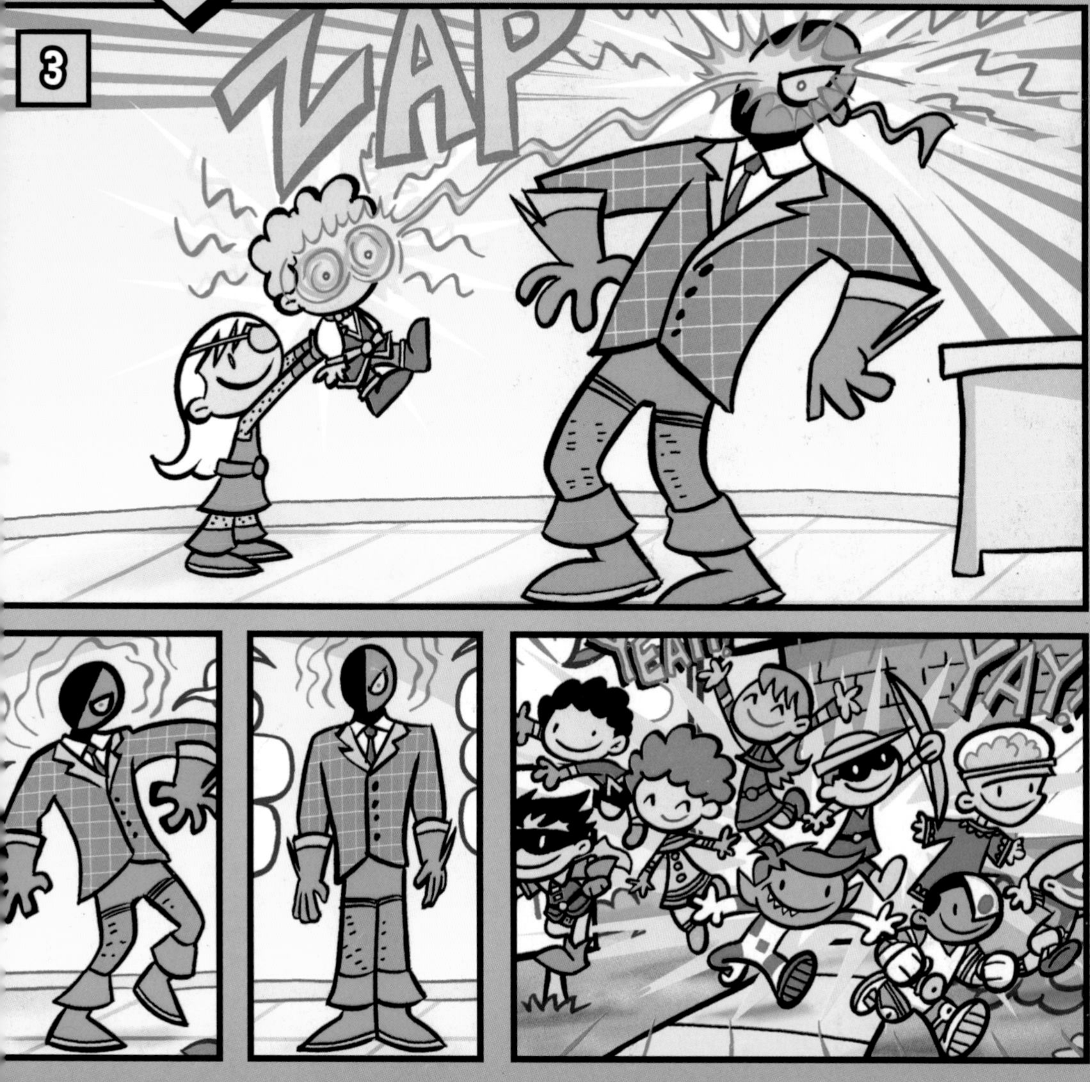
3
ZAP
YEAH!
YAY!

tiny titans

FIND COOL WEBSITES AND MORE BOOKS LIKE THIS ONE AT WWW.FACTHOUND.COM.
JUST TYPE IN THE BOOK ID: 9781434245397

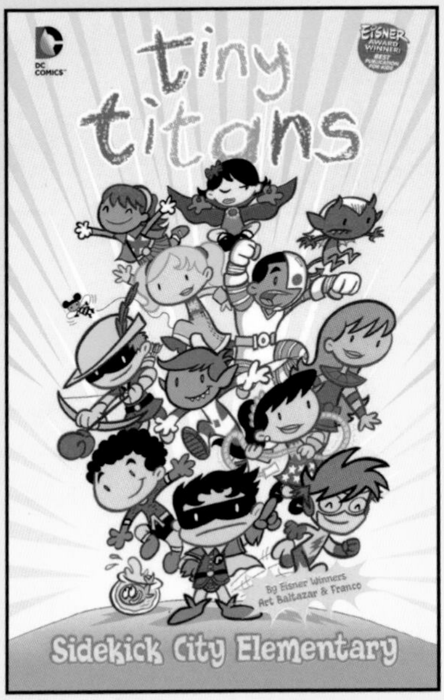
DC COMICS
tiny titans
By Eisner Winners Art Baltazar & Franco
Sidekick City Elementary

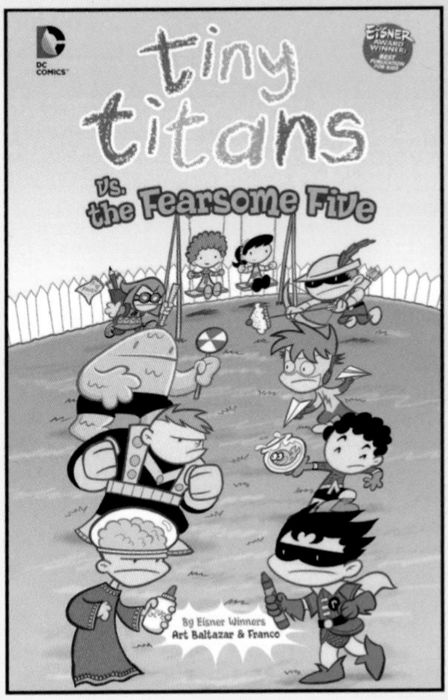
DC COMICS
tiny titans
vs. the Fearsome Five
By Eisner Winners Art Baltazar & Franco

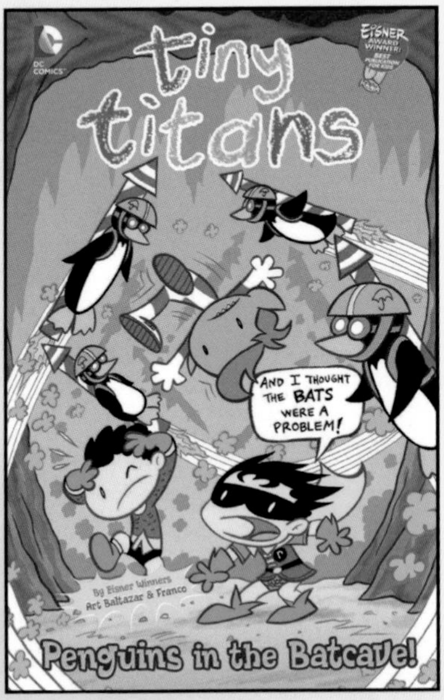
DC COMICS
tiny titans
AND I THOUGHT THE BATS WERE A PROBLEM!
By Eisner Winners Art Baltazar & Franco
Penguins in the Batcave!

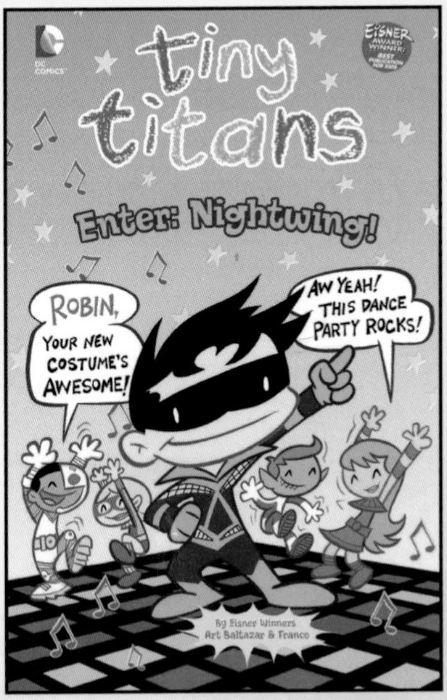
DC COMICS
tiny titans
Enter: Nightwing!
ROBIN, YOUR NEW COSTUME'S AWESOME!
AW YEAH! THIS DANCE PARTY ROCKS!
By Eisner Winners Art Baltazar & Franco

WANT EVEN MORE COMICS?

TO FIND A COMICS SHOP NEAR YOU:
CALL 1-888 COMIC BOOK
OR VISIT WWW.COMICSHOPLOCATOR.COM